And in the **MORNING**

And in the
MORNING

JOHN WILSON

KIDS CAN PRESS

Kids Can Press acknowledges the financial support of the Ontario Arts Council, the Canada Council for the Arts and the Government of Canada, through the BPIDP, for our publishing activity.

Published in Canada by
Kids Can Press Ltd.
29 Birch Avenue
Toronto, ON M4V 1E2

Published in the U.S. by
Kids Can Press Ltd.
2250 Military Road
Tonawanda, NY 14150

www.kidscanpress.com

Edited by Charis Wahl
Cover and interior designed by Karen Powers
Cover photo of Richard Symons Hay (top) courtesy John Wilson.
Cover photo (bottom) courtesy Imperial War Museum/E(AUS)846.
Printed and bound in Canada

CM 03 0 9 8 7 6 5 4 3 2 1
CM PA 03 0 9 8 7 6 5 4 3 2 1

National Library of Canada Cataloguing in Publication Data

Wilson, John (John Alexander), 1951–
    And in the morning / John Wilson.

ISBN 1-55337-400-2 (bound). ISBN 1-55337-348-0 (pbk.)

1. Great Britain. Army. Highland Light Infantry, 16th — Fiction.
I. Title.

PS8595.I5834A85 2003   jC813'.54   C2002-903033-1
PZ7

Kids Can Press is a *l©rus*™ Entertainment company

✤ ✤ ✤

For Private Richard Symons Hay, S/14143
7th Battalion Cameron Highlanders

Born: Ayr, Scotland
Killed in action: 25 September 1915,
Loos, Belgium

My great-grandfather gave me a gift when I turned sixteen, even though he died the year I was born. My father had tucked away the package, and there it was on my birthday, almost hidden amongst all the bigger, brightly coloured presents. It was wrapped in plain brown paper, tied with old, yellowed string, and it smelled vaguely musty.

It was only later, after all the excitement was over and I was sitting in my room, that I remembered it. I doubted that the grey-haired old man in the family album could give me anything interesting, but I picked at the knotted string, just for something to do.

Beneath the wrapping was a diary with PRIVATE in black ink on the soft leather cover. The pages were covered in small, neat handwriting; and stuffed between them were letters, newspaper cuttings, documents and one old photograph faded brown, on heavy paper, and about the size of a postcard. In the photograph, a soldier stood very stiffly, staring straight at the camera. He was wearing a soft cap with some sort of badge on it, a jacket with four large pockets and a kilt.

I put the photo on the shelf above my bed and opened the diary. In the front was a letter that looked fairly recent, written in a wide, shaky hand. It was addressed to me.

7

Dear Jim,

I hope you are reading this on your sixteenth birthday. You are a baby now and I shall not live to see you much older, but by the time you read this, you will be old enough to understand.

This diary and these letters and cuttings are the story of another Jim. When he started writing, he was your age. You will find wonderful and terrible things in these pages, about Jim and the strange world he lived in. But you will learn about yourself, too. Every family has secrets. Ours is no different. One secret concerns the lad who wrote this diary.

Good luck,

Robert

Tuesday, August 4, 1914

It's going to be war! Germany has invaded Belgium! Unless they stop, we will be at war by tomorrow. It is all anyone can talk about.

Yesterday, Mother, Father and I took the train to the beach at Largs for the Bank Holiday. My friend Iain came with us. He lives with his elderly Aunt Sadie, who is a delightful character but has no time for the holiday crowds at the seaside. The beach was crowded — even war cannot prevent a Bank Holiday — and the water superbly cold after our time in the hot sun. The carriage on the train back to Paisley was full of brave soldiers hurrying to report to their depots for service. They were so cheerful and ardent, smoking, laughing and singing songs. With the exception of "Tipperary," Mother did not wish us to listen closely to the words. Father was unusually quiet. He is in the reserves, so his call-up papers will arrive any day now. Then he will get his chance.

What an adventure this war is, and so close on the heels of Shackleton's departure to cross the Great Frozen Antarctic Continent. Shackleton is my hero, but even his noble enterprise cannot compare to this! I am so excited I can barely sit still long enough to write this page — but I must. I promised I would begin a diary this summer, and what better day to begin than this???

GREAT BRITAIN DECLARES WAR ON GERMANY

HUGE CROWDS CHEER THEIR MAJESTIES AT PALACE

Owing to the summary rejection by the German Government of the request made by his Majesty's Government for assurances that the neutrality of Belgium would be respected, his Majesty's Government has declared to the German Government that a state of war exists between Great Britain and Germany.

Shortly after the declaration, His Majesty King George and Queen Mary stepped onto the balcony at Buckingham Palace to a huge reception of cheering and singing from the assembled crowd. Never in history has this nation entered into such a momentous undertaking with such enthusiasm and resolve.

Wednesday, August 5

THE FIRST NAVAL ACTION OF THE WAR. The news–boys were shouting it through the streets. This morning, the destroyer *Amphion* came upon a German mine–layer, the *Konigin Luise,* and sank her. It is a small engagement, but it will serve notice that the Royal Navy is about and not to be trifled with.

Father's call–up papers arrived this morning — a policeman brought the telegram first thing. I desperately wanted to be the one to give him the telegram, so I rushed to the door, but Father must have been waiting. He was reading it as I tore around the corner in the hall, and I thought he looked oddly sad. However, he brightened when he saw me.

"Well, young Jimmy," he said, "I'm to be a soldier again."

"That's wonderful," I blurted out. "I hope the war goes on long enough for me to have a turn."

"Yes," he said quietly, "but they say it will be over soon. I expect I shall be back to eat Christmas dinner with you and Mother."

I heard a sob and turned in time to see Mother's back disappearing into the parlour. Father ruffled my hair and followed her, closing the door after him. Why isn't everyone else as happy as I am?

I listened at the parlour door. I had to!

"Why do you want to throw away a good job to be a shilling-a-day soldier?" Mother was asking.

"First of all," Father replied, "they will hold my job for me. I don't expect I shall be away for long. The French may even finish off the Germans before I get there.

"Second, I have no choice. Look what it says. If I do not present myself at once, I will be 'liable to be proceeded against.' Would you rather see me in jail?"

"I'd rather see you alive in jail than dead on some battlefield."

There was no more talking, just the sound of Mother crying. What's the matter with her? Doesn't she see the Glory of it all? Why must she spoil Father's

ARMY RESERVE

(REGULAR RESERVE ONLY)

GENERAL MOBILIZATION

Notice to Join the Army for Permanent Service

Name _William Peter Hay_ Rank _Second Lieutenant_

Regimental Number _G/1513_

You are hereby required to join

the 2nd Battalion, Highland Light Infantry

at _Argyll Barracks, Glasgow_ on _AT ONCE_

Should you not present yourself on that day, you will be liable to be proceeded against.

You will bring with you your "Small Book," your Life Certificate, Identity Certificate, and, if a Regular Reservist, Parchment Reserve Certificate.

Instructions for obtaining the sum of 3s. as an advance of pay and a Travelling Warrant where necessary, are contained in your Identity Certificate.

If your Identity Certificate is not in your possession and you are unable to proceed to join, you must report at once to this office, either personally or by letter.

Stamp of the Officer i/c Records.

departure? I wish I could go. But I am only sixteen (or will be, in a week). Three years before I can join up, and it will all be over by then.

IT IS SO UNFAIR!

✣   ✣   ✣

We went to the station this afternoon to see Father off on the Glasgow train. The excitement in the air was almost unbearable. The streets were crowded, even though it is a weekday, and there were flags everywhere. Down the High Street to the Cross was a sea of flat caps and summer bonnets, with occasional parasols standing out like small sailboats. Groups of men stood on every street corner, talking and buying the latest special edition of the *Daily Mail* to find out what was happening in Belgium.

The train was full of soldiers, clamouring at the windows, saying goodbye and shouting. The atmosphere was so cheerful. It was as if they were setting off on a holiday excursion. How I wish I were going with them!

Mother cried most embarrassingly, and I was afraid she would break down completely. Fortunately, there were other distraught women on the platform, so she did not stand out too much.

Father dried Mother's tears and said he would be back before she knew it. He took her aside, out of my hearing, and talked to her very seriously and firmly for a few minutes. Mother just nodded and dabbed at her eyes. Then Father spoke to me.

"Well, Jimmy," he said, "I am leaving you with a lot of responsibility while I am gone."

I felt myself stand up straighter at that.

"Mother is going to find the next few weeks difficult," he went on. "She is fragile, so I want you to be well-behaved and to help her around the house as much as possible." I nodded. "And don't rush to join up."

"But I'm too young," I protested.

"That may be," Father said, his face tense, "but I don't think that's stopping many people these days. I do not have a choice, but you do. War is not the big adventure some would have you believe. Only a fool or a fanatic would rush to war. You are not a fool, but this is a fanatical time. Promise me you will think carefully and not do anything rash."

"I will."

Father's face relaxed. "I will write you both letters whenever I can, and I want to read in your mother's letters to me that you have been a big help."

"I will be," I said very seriously, "but I wish I were going, too."

"You're too young," Father said with a smile, "but I can bring you back a souvenir. What would you like?"

"A German helmet," I said immediately. "One of those ones with the spike on top." Father's smile broadened. "See if you can get one with a bullet hole through it."

"I'll see what I can do," he said, but his smile had faded. Then he ruffled my hair, kissed Mother and boarded the train. We watched until the last carriage disappeared, long after Father was out of sight.

Since we have returned home, Mother has shut herself in her room. I heard sobbing through the door when I knocked to see how she was. We had a supper laid out in the cold pantry, so I ate that. I took some cuts of meat in to her, but she has not touched them. I hope she will be better after some sleep.

DESTROYER AMPHION SUNK
GREAT LOSS OF LIFE

The destroyer *Amphion* sank this morning, minutes after striking one of the mines laid by the *Konigin Luise* yesterday. One hundred and thirty men went down with her. However, twenty German sailors who had been rescued by the *Amphion* when the *Konigin Luise* went down were locked in the destroyer's brig and also perished.

Thursday, August 6

Mines are such a cowardly way to wage war. But what can one expect from Germans?

Kitchener of Khartoum has been named Minister of War. He will show the Kaiser what's what!

The gallant Belgians have won a great victory at Liège. The Huns were shot down in such numbers that the walls of their dead threatened to block the firing of the great guns of the fort. Why are they so stupid? The

German army will be stuck before the forts at Liège and Namur until our Expeditionary Force and the French come up and push them back to Berlin where they belong. Father is right. It will all be over very soon.

The *Daily Mail* has recommended that readers refuse service from German or Austrian waiters in restaurants. It has also printed a map of the continent. I am going to pin mine up on my wall and mark the progress of our armies — ON TO BERLIN.

Mother came out of her room today. She looks tired, and I have seen tears when she thought I was not looking. I have tried to help as much as I can.

Friday, August 7

I walked around the town for a while today. Not as busy as previously, but still a sense of excitement in the air. Recruiting posters have appeared everywhere.

Rally Round the Flag, Boys
EVERY FIT MAN WANTED

The newspapers say that even the socialists are supporting the war. So much for all their pacifist talk. One of them, I forget his name, was shot in Paris for speaking out against the war. How can anyone not be excited?

The army has opened a recruiting office in the High Street, and the line-up of men waiting to join stretched all the way down the hill to the Abbey. They are so lucky. I came home feeling very low. Mother says I should be glad. She says that war is a horrible thing, and no good ever comes of it. She doesn't understand. Of course people get hurt in war. Some will lose limbs, some will even perish, but that is the excitement. Conquering the foe would be meaningless if there was no danger at all. WHEN WILL MY TURN COME?

Saturday, August 8

The French have gone on the offensive! Yesterday morning, they tore down the border posts and marched into their stolen province of Alsace. They took Altkirch in a wild bayonet charge, and it is said they will be in Mulhouse by now. What a wonderful moment — the French cavalry in their gleaming breastplates, the infantry soldiers in their blue and red uniforms, gloriously getting revenge for their defeat in the last war. What made the Hun think he could win this time?

Now that I have begun my diary, I am enjoying it. Far from it being the chore I feared, I look forward to sitting at the end of the day and recording what has happened. It clears my mind, and these are momentous times. Perhaps I will read it as an old man in 1950! Hello, Jim. How's your lumbago?

Perhaps someday someone else will be interested. I wonder.

I suppose that if posterity may take an interest in my ramblings, I should say something about myself. My name is Jim Hay. My father calls me Jimmy, but everyone else calls me Jim.

I will be sixteen years old next Wednesday (August 12). My best friend is Iain Scott, and I am in love with Anne Cunningham. Should I say this sort of thing? Well, I have. So no one must read this. I should have bought a diary with a lock.

Father is an engineer and works in the locomotive sheds, building engines that are sent to our colonies all over the world. Some are even chugging about India.

I am an only child, and I arrived after my parents had been married for almost twenty years. That makes them quite old, so I never knew my grandparents. In fact, apart from my parents, I have no family at all.

As a young man, Father joined the army to fight in Africa in the Boer War. He doesn't talk about it, but he must have done very well because he was made a lieutenant and won medals. It is because he went to that war that he is in the reserves now and has been called up. Of course, he would have volunteered anyway.

Even though she is old, Mother is beautiful. Her skin is very pale and she is thin and fragile. I almost think she would break if she fell over. But, when she dresses up for a special occasion, or even just for church on Sundays, she is radiant and I am so proud.

Mother suffers from nerves. That is why I have to look after her while Father is away. Once, when I was little, I had a very bad fever. Mother suffered from her nerves so much that she took to her bed for two whole days. Mother sometimes has these attacks — hysterics, Father calls them. I hope she doesn't have one while Father is away.

Sunday, August 9

A terrible day. I find it hard to write about.

Mother could not find her purse before we left for church. She is normally so careful, and she is NEVER late for anything. We searched all over. Mother became quite flustered. Eventually the purse turned up on the dressing table — I don't know how she could have missed it — but we were late for church, and everyone turned and looked as we entered.

During the service, the minister told us about the atrocities the Huns are committing in Belgium — burning towns, shooting innocent people. Even nuns are being murdered and babies skewered on bayonets. How can a supposedly civilized people stoop to such depths? It was all quite beastly. I sent up a silent prayer that Father and the rest of our army hurry over to teach the barbarians a lesson they will not soon forget.

I walked with Anne after church. She was quite upset by the minister's words. I wonder if he should talk of such things in front of the fair sex.

We walked down by the old mill on the river. I'm afraid I must have monopolized the conversation. I was angry about the poor Belgians and went on about the need to get our army over there to exact retribution.

Anne just listened. She is not enthusiastic about the war.

When we got to the mill, there was a group of boys near the water. Some were from my school. Albert Tomkins was there, and the biggest boy, the leader, was Hugh McLean. He's a tough boy from the Glasgow slums by the docks. His father was killed in an accident in the shipyards, so he lives with his grandmother here in Paisley. That's probably the only reason he wasn't working. He certainly learns very little at school.

When Anne and I reached the bank, we suddenly had a clear view of what was going on. Hugh and the others were gathered around a rough arena made of old pieces of wood. In the centre was one of the largest brown rats I have ever seen. Rats are common around the mill — they feed on the spilled grain — but this one was huge.

Each boy had a sharpened stick. They were poking the rat and shouting.

"Take that, you Hun baby-killer!"

"This is just a taste of what our boys'll give you when they get over there!"

"Get back to Berlin where you belong!"

The rat was exhausted. Its fur was matted, there was blood coming from one side of its mouth, and one of its eyes was gone. But it was still fighting, biting at the sticks that were tormenting it.

As we watched, Hugh stuck his stick into the rat's side. The poor creature twitched violently, desperate to wriggle off the point. Hugh grinned over at me and Anne, and let out a rough laugh. "That's whit ah'm gonnie dae tae ony oh' they Germans that gets in ma way."

Anne let out a gasp and ran. I caught up to her by the roadside. She was sobbing uncontrollably. I didn't know what to say, but knew I should say something. I chose the wrong thing.

"It's only a rat."

Anne turned on me. Her eyes were a fury.

"Only a rat!" she shouted. "Yes, it is only a rat, and the Belgians are only babies and nuns, and the soldiers are only boys. Is this what you want your precious war to do — turn us all into animals who torture defenceless creatures until we are ready to kill one another?"

Tears were streaming down Anne's cheeks. For a moment I thought she was going to fall forward against me. I hoped she would. All I wanted to do was put my arms around her and comfort her. But then I opened my stupid mouth again.

"Anne," I stammered. "We cannot let the Germans march through Belgium. We must teach them a lesson. You must understand that."

"Understand! I understand!" she shouted. "You are a fool, James Hay. You will go off to war like all the rest. I don't want you to end up like that poor rat."

With that, she pushed my chest. I staggered back and Anne strode off down the road.

What had she meant? I wasn't going to end up like that rat. How could she not be in favour of the war?

For the rest of the day, I just moped around. I hope tomorrow will be better.

HUNS STUCK AT LIÈGE

The mighty Belgian fortress of Liège is proving a tough nut for the Kaiser to crack. For days now, von Moltke's Prussian armies have been beating at the door. The proud Belgians will not let them in. These mighty works can never be taken by frontal assault. The Hun will simply wear himself out on their slopes.

Monday, August 10

I do not feel much better, and the news is not good. The Germans have surrounded Antwerp, and the French have retreated from Mulhouse after some hard fighting. The forts at Liège still hold.

Iain and I went along the High Street today. There are still long lines at the recruiting office. As we passed the door, Hugh McLean and Albert Tomkins came out wearing smiles as wide as the River Clyde.

"What were you doing in there?" Iain asked.

"Joinin' up, o' course. Whit dae yeh think we wis daen'?" answered Hugh in his thick Glasgow accent.

Hugh is very rough and could easily pass for eighteen or nineteen.

"But you're not old enough," I blurted out.

Hugh laughed. "Ah'm auld enough fer this adventure," he said. "Anyhoo, they dinnae care. There wis a lad afore me, nae mare'n fourteen. Tells the sergent he wis sixteen, the eejit. Sergent looks him up an' doon.

'Take a walk aroon' the park fer hauf an oor, lad, an' come back when yer nineteen.' That's the way it is. If ye want tae go, ye can."

"When're you boys joinin' up?" Albert asked.

"Not just yet," I said, and had to look down at the pavement. Hugh joining up was one thing. He never fitted in at school, always telling us he should be working in the shipyards on the Clyde instead of stuck here in Paisley. But Albert! He is the same age as me and looks even younger. He is tall enough, but he is thin, weedy and pale. He will gloat horribly over going while Iain and I are not.

"Ah weel," Hugh said, swaggering down the road with Albert traipsing alongside, "be sure and no' leave it tae late. Yon war'll nae be goin' on tae long after ah'm over there."

Iain and I watched them disappear into the crowd. The temptation to join the long line of men was almost unbearable. Why should the likes of Hugh and Albert have all the fun?

I believe that if either of us had said a single word just then, we would have ended up in the recruiting office and worried about the consequences later. But neither of us did. For the longest time, we watched the line file slowly through the door. Then we drifted down the High Street towards the Abbey.

I cannot speak for Iain, but what held me back were Anne's words yesterday. I am still confused by them. Before I do anything, I will have to sort that mess out.

When we reached the Abbey, we sat on a flat moss-covered gravestone. The date on it was 1764. I told Iain about Hugh and the rat.

"He'll come to no good, that one," Iain said. "If anyone has to take a German bayonet, I hope it's Hugh."

"Iain!" I was shocked, but deep inside, I shared his wish.

"You're mad about Anne, aren't you?" Iain changed the topic.

"Yes," I admitted. "There's something … special about her."

"Have you kissed her?" he asked.

"No," I replied.

"Do you want to?"

"Of course I do!"

"Then do it," he said. "And do it soon. She may be right about this war changing us all, and whether we join up now or wait, we will have to go and do our bit. Don't go without kissing her."

Iain is a full year older than me and knows a lot more about women than I do. He was held back at school for a year — that's why he is in my class. It's not that he is stupid, but he grew up in India, and the schools there are different. He arrived a year ago, able to speak fluent Urdu but unable to do the maths we were working on. Apparently his parents both died of cholera, so he was sent to live with his Aunt Sadie and finish his schooling here in Paisley. We became friends almost instantly.

Iain is taller than me by about three inches. He has an unkempt shock of brown hair and skin burnt dark by the sun. Of course, that is not what Hugh says. He taunts Iain with "tar baby" and says he has a "touch of the tar brush" in him. Iain ignores Hugh. Insults have a way of sliding off him. With me, they burrow deep and fester. I don't know what I would do without Iain for a friend.

"Should we join up?" I asked.

At length, he said, "I was wondering that. I want to do my bit, and I think the Germans do need to be taught a lesson. They can't just go storming wherever they want without so much as a by-your-leave." He thought a bit, then said, "If the war lasts long enough, I will go. But when I do, I want it to be my decision, not just being swept up in the rush.

"Besides," he went on, turning towards me and smiling, "I can't leave you behind, and you have to stay at least until you fix it all up with that Anne of yours." He gave me a friendly pat on the arm. "Let's let Hugh have his turn first. I doubt if the Germans have ever met anyone like him."

"Or Albert," I added. "I doubt if he is strong enough to lift his rifle."

Laughing, we headed back up the High Street, arm in arm. Iain helped me feel a bit better, but I do have to sort things out with Anne. Why is life so complicated?

Tuesday, August 11

The Belgians are surprising everyone with their bravery in holding up the Germans. The French don't seem to be going anywhere. Where is our army?

Went round to Anne's today, but she was not home. Is she avoiding me? I cannot stop thinking about her.

Anne and her father came over from Canada ten or eleven years ago. He is a free thinker and a strong socialist and was in some kind of trouble over there. According to Anne, he was the leader of a strike at one of the steel plants near Toronto. The bosses brought in the militia and there was fighting. Anne's mother had died of consumption the year before, and her father didn't want to raise Anne in the midst of violence, so he moved here to work in the shipyards. He is still a socialist — he has some strange notions — but he doesn't lead strikes anymore. Anne has picked up some of his ideas and is quite outspoken. I don't understand some of the things she talks about, but I admire her courage tremendously. She is also very beautiful. She has long hair the colour of gold, and the most wonderful deep-green eyes. I hope she has forgiven me for our fight.

Mother continues to be forgetful. Today she lost her favourite hair clasp, and we spent a full hour looking for it before it turned up in a kitchen drawer. Mother got quite cross and accused me of hiding it, but I have no idea how it got there.

Birthday tomorrow. Too excited to write more.

Wednesday, August 12

MY BIRTHDAY! At last, I am sixteen, an important step closer to joining the army — although, if what Hugh says is true, I could go right now.

Not many presents, but all very special. The best was a card from Father to say he has arrived at the barracks in England safely. He said that by the time we get this, he will be on his way south to get a helmet for me.

Mother and Father gave me a pocket watch of my very own. Mother said she hadn't had a chance to have it engraved, but she will. She cried when I thanked her. She is very emotional these days.

There was another present from Father, which he bought before he left. It is a box kite, the largest one I have ever seen. It will fly wonderfully, but there was no wind today. Father's accompanying letter said he couldn't decide between this or a set of Meccano, fresh from Mr. Hornby's new factory in Liverpool. He decided on the kite because it would get me out in the fresh air.

Iain came round. He got me a new book from America by someone named Burroughs. It is called *Tarzan of the Apes*. I hope it is good. I have just finished Jack London's *White Fang*, so am looking for something to read.

Anne came by as well. Her gift was also a book, *Beasts and Superbeasts*, the new collection of stories by Saki. Anne and I went for a walk. She apologized for her outburst at the river, but said she cannot abide cruelty, even to a rat. The war is bothering her as much as it is exciting everyone else.

"I'm sorry, too," I said. "I didn't like seeing the rat tortured either. I am so excited by war news that I suppose I'm not thinking too clearly."

"That's the whole problem," Anne replied. "Everyone, from the Kaiser and Kitchener all the way down to you, is too excited to think clearly. No one is even allowed to criticize the war —"

"Of course not. It's unpatriotic," I interrupted.

"What's unpatriotic is stopping people from saying what they think and feel. Oh, Jim, the whole world has gone mad. Only a month ago, people were worried about the unrest in Ireland. They were planning holidays, thinking about money, living their lives. Now it's all been turned upside down. Ireland's been forgotten and millions of men are trying to kill one another. I'm so frightened."

Anne's eyes were filling with tears — she looked so beautiful. Girls just don't understand war, but I knew that if I tried to explain, she would storm off again — and that was the last thing I wanted.

I put my arm around Anne and she rested her head on my shoulder. I could feel her hair against my cheek. I wanted to kiss her, and had almost plucked up the courage to try, when she suddenly pulled away and looked straight at me. "Promise me that you won't do anything stupid like lying about your age and joining the army."

I was a bit taken aback — how could she know what was in my mind? I stuttered something about Iain and I waiting. Was that a promise? I don't know. More complications.

When Anne went home, she kissed me. It was a very quick brush of her lips on my cheek, but my skin felt on fire. I long to kiss her properly.

DECISIVE BATTLE OUTSIDE LOUVAIN

GERMAN BODIES COVER THE GROUND

German cavalry advancing on the ancient Belgian town of Louvain received an unpleasant surprise yesterday. At Haelen, they met General de Witte and were stopped cold by the well-placed Belgian machine guns. The Germans retired, leaving the field covered with the bodies of their dead.

Thursday, August 13

Great news from Haelen. Everyone's sure the Huns will retire with their tails between their legs now. The war will be over by Christmas after all! I do hope our soldiers get there in time to be a part of the great victory march to Berlin.

A cartoon in *Punch* has summed up the mood perfectly. Above the caption "NO THOROUGHFARE!" is a picture of brave little Belgium as a small wooden-shoed boy barring the farm gate before the fat old Hun bandmaster, complete with a string of sausages hanging from his pocket. I did laugh. I have pinned it to the wall beside my map.

MAMMOTH GERMAN SIEGE GUNS POUND LIÈGE FORTS

Guns of a size never before seen in the history of war opened fire on the forts around Liège yesterday. Within hours, all the forts east of the city fell, some of their brave defenders driven out of their minds from the concussion of the explosions. The remaining forts are not expected to hold out long.

Friday, August 14

Why is good news always followed by bad? Where are our soldiers? There is no word in the *Daily Mail* or the *Glasgow Herald*, and I read both the morning and evening editions.

Saturday, August 15

The French are attacking again, this time in Lorraine. This is the real thing. The remaining forts at Liège are still resisting the German guns.

I finished *Tarzan of the Apes* today. It is quite exciting, but a bit silly. Perhaps real life is just so much more thrilling.

Sunday, August 16

Church this morning and a walk with Anne. We did not go down by the mill, and I tried my hardest not to mention the war. Luckily, Anne suggested that we go to the park, where they had set up a mobile biograph in a tent. For a halfpenny, we saw a newsreel and two moving-picture shows. The newsreel showed soldiers, ours and the French, marching and getting on and off trains. There were some pictures of guns firing, but they could have been anywhere. I was disappointed that there was no film of fighting, but I did not say so.

The films were a new episode of the *Perils of Pauline* and a comedy from Keystone, *Mabel at the Wheel*. Mabel Norman is one of my favourites. There was a new actor in it, Charlie Chaplin. He played the villain, but he had one very funny bit where Mabel falls off his motorbike into a puddle.

Chaplin is English and seems to be doing quite well in America. Anne said that she would like to go back to Canada. She told me what little she remembers about skating on frozen rivers and having picnics by the lakes north of Toronto. I am not sure about ice skating, but I love picnics. I could almost see Anne and me sitting with a hamper on a rug by the lakeshore. There are beavers working on their dams, colourful woodpeckers busy on the tree trunks and a canoe waiting for us on the shore. The sun is bright and hot, and the leaves are deep reds and golds. Might I be seeing our future? I hope so.

"After the war," I said, "I'll take you to Toronto and we will have a picnic by a lake." Anne smiled at that, but there was sadness in her eyes.

I returned home to find Mother polishing the silver. Hadn't she done it just last week? But she told me it was tarnished. She was still at it when I came in here to write my diary.

The evening papers were all about the fall of the last forts at Liège. There is now nothing between von Kluck's armies and Brussels. The poor, noble Belgians. At least Japan has declared for the Allies. That will allow the Russians to move more of their army against the German east.

The whole world is fighting against Germany and Austria. Our Expeditionary Force will be joined by men from all over the Empire. Canada, Australia, New Zealand, India — even the Irish are said to be flocking to the colours.

I can still hear Mother cleaning the silver.

Monday, August 17

The French continue to attack, but take heavy casualties. It is all so frustrating.

Nothing seems to matter but the war, and it feels so dull here now that great events are happening on the continent. But still no word from Father or of our Expeditionary Force. Not even any wind to fly my kite.

Mother is fine today, cheerful and talkative. We had a pleasant stroll this evening after she returned from work. We did not mention the war once.

Tuesday, August 18

The Russians are on the move. Their main army crossed the border into Prussia yesterday. Everyone is surprised, particularly the Germans, I imagine, at how fast they have mobilized their army of peasants. Another sign that things are not going the Huns' way.

The war has been going on for two whole weeks now and no word of what our soldiers are doing. I can only hope that the news is being held secret from the newspapers. After all, we don't want old von Kluck finding out what we intend by reading the *Glasgow Herald*. All the same, it is frustrating not to know.

The announcements of the French advance in Lorraine are very exciting, but when I searched them for names of major towns to mark on my map, I didn't find any. It is puzzling.

Good breeze this afternoon, so Iain and I took the box kite to the park. I was right about it flying wonderfully — as soon as it took flight, it positively soared into the sky, heading for the puffy little clouds amongst the perfect blue. Iain was asking for his turn to fly it when we heard a voice.

"Hey you! Take that thing down. Don't you know there's a war on?"

We looked around to see a large policeman sweating his way over the grass.

"Yes, sir, we know," I answered. "We are just flying my new kite. It was a present from my father. He's in the army."

"Then he would not be too happy if his son was mistaken for a German spy signalling to thae Zeppelin things."

"We're not spies," Iain said.

"I daresay yer not," the policeman replied, "but it's not everyone will know that. Why, just yesterday a man was beaten 'alf to death down in England because the crowd thought he was a spy cutting telegraph wires."

"Was he?" I asked eagerly.

"Not at all. He was from the local council, fixing the wires, not cutting them. But if the police hadn't showed up, he would be dead for sure. So just take it down to be on the safe side."

We hauled the kite down, annoyed that we could not go on with our game but thrilled that there might be spies in our own town. It is such an exciting time.

Wednesday, August 19

A COMMUNIQUÉ FROM OUR EXPEDITIONARY FORCE! They have landed and are rushing to the Front. At last! How I wish I were there.

The Russians continue their advance. I hope the Russian Bear is as huge as everyone says because I do not think their soldiers are very good as individuals, being mostly illiterate.

PEASANT SOLDIERS SHOOT AT OWN AIRCRAFT

An unanticipated problem has arisen amongst the vast Russian army, at this moment rolling into Germany. Many Russian soldiers have never come in contact with modern technology. At the sight of any airplane, they blaze away, apparently convinced that such a wonderful invention cannot be anything other than German.

Thursday, August 20

BRUSSELS HAS FALLEN. Poor little Belgium. She has stood up magnificently to the Teutonic bully, but she is too small. I hope it will not be long before we can give her her freedom back.

On a brighter note, the French are attacking victoriously all along their frontier. Iain and I met Hugh McLean in town today. He is as cocky as ever. He took great glee in telling us that he and Albert have to report to barracks tomorrow. Apparently there are so many volunteers that there is talk of forming a unit just from Paisley. There are several already forming in Glasgow, one made up entirely of employees of the Tramways Corporation! If only I could go. Will Hugh's and Albert's seats be the only empty ones when school starts? How are we expected to take school work seriously with such momentous events happening?

Boulogne, August 18

Dearest Jimmy,

Well, here I am in la belle France. The trip over the Channel was a bit rough, everyone but yours truly being seasick. I suspect it was from the smell of the horses below decks as much as the weather. We all perked up the moment we marched down the gangway. We were welcomed with shouts of "Vive les Anglais!" Small boys ran along beside our column, calling out for chocolate and cigarettes, and mademoiselles threw flowers at us. I think I shall like this country.

How is your mother? Are you helping her? Have you had a chance to fly your kite yet?

I will write again when I can.

Father

Friday, August 21

A card from Father! It showed the sea front at Boulogne and was posted the evening before they all set off to their congregation point on the Belgian frontier. Mother did not seem very happy to get the card.

The French continue to fight all along their line. Why are they not breaking through? The Russians have won a stunning victory at Gumbinnen. Perhaps the peasant soldiers are not as stupid as we think?

Saturday, August 22

A CAVALRY ENGAGEMENT! Our men saw off a party of Uhlans, the German cavalry, at a place called Soignes, in Belgium. The first time our troops have been in battle and they were victorious.

I looked up Soignes on my map. It is near a town called Mons. I wonder if that is where Father is. The French are fighting heavily around Charleroi. That is near Mons, too. Is Father in battle already?

Mother polished the silver again this evening. It was not tarnished at all. Father's card has set her back to the odd mood she was in of late. I hope she is not getting sick.

BRITISH TROOPS ENGAGED AT MONS

Today British troops were engaged on European soil for the first time since Waterloo, ninety-nine years ago. Units of

General French's Expeditionary Force were dug in along a canal near the Belgian town of Mons when they were attacked by the full might of von Kluck's army, 200,000 men according to some reports.

Our superbly trained men gave a stirring account of themselves and bloodied the Germans' noses. The Germans attacked in close order across open ground, and our men, with fine discipline and accurate, rapid fire, mowed them down in hundreds. There is no word yet as to casualties, but it will be a long time before the Germans think to attack our lads again.

Sunday, August 23

A GREAT BATTLE. I wonder if Father has my helmet yet? Tomorrow our Expeditionary Force will attack and drive the Huns back where they belong.

The weather continues superb. Walked in the sunshine with Anne after church. She held my hand, and we did not talk about the war once. We planned a picnic for next Sunday. It is not by a lake in Canada, but a local stream will do nicely for now. I am very excited. Perhaps I will kiss her!

Monday, August 24

OUR ARMY IS IN RETREAT!!! How can this be? They were victorious yesterday. Apparently the French 5th Army withdrew, leaving our right flank open to attack. We had to withdraw to close the line. Let us hope it is only a minor setback.

Tuesday, August 25

The retreat continues. Mother very distracted. She mislaid her purse again this morning and refused to go to work until she found it. It took a full hour before I came upon it behind a chair in the drawing room. How did it end up there? Mother was late for work.

Wednesday, August 26

Our Expeditionary Force fought today at Le Cateau. The Germans have not learned and again came at our soldiers in waves, like targets at the Fun Fair. Is the retreat over?

MYSTERIOUS OCCURRENCE AT MONS

Reports are filtering through of supernatural sightings during the recent battle at Mons and the subsequent withdrawal of our army. According to several eyewitnesses, at the height of the battle, a line of ghostly bowmen appeared between the opposing forces. These apparitions, dressed in clothing from the time of the Battle of Agincourt, the site of which is not too far distant from Mons, fired shining arrows at the charging Germans, who, despite no visible sign of injury, dropped down dead.

Subsequently, winged angels appeared in the sky above our troops. The angels did not communicate with our men, but all who saw them reported being almost overwhelmed by a feeling of well-being and comfort.

Thursday, August 27

The Russians are engaged in a fierce battle around a place called Tannenberg. It is not yet clear who is winning. The paper this evening reported that the retreating Germans have been leaving behind spies dressed as peasant women. Several have been discovered by the Russians because, although convincingly dressed, they wear army-issue underwear!

Our army is retreating again. The bulletins call it a withdrawal, but there is no other word but retreat. It is so humiliating. If this goes on, the Huns will be in Paris in a few days.

Iain came round today. We are both feeling low. I fear I might be coming down with a cold.

Friday, August 28

Feeling most unwell. Mother told me to stay in bed this morning. When she returned from work this afternoon, she asked why I was lying in bed and could not remember telling me to stay there. I am really quite worried about her. I am very proud of Father, but I wish he were here.

Saturday, August 29

Still unwell. Anne visited but did not stay long. I am not much company. We have postponed our picnic for a week.

Sunday, August 30

A little better, but still in bed all day. My state not helped by the news. The retreat goes on in France, and the Russian army has been destroyed at Tannenberg. All our optimism has vanished. It may be a short war, but it will end with the Kaiser walking down the Champs Elysées! I am feeling very low.

GERMANS SACK LOUVAIN
WOMEN AND CHILDREN SHOT

In new proof of Hun brutality, the mediaeval town of Louvain has been put to the torch. As the flames consumed the priceless library and its 230,000 books, drunken soldiers cavorted in the hellish, flickering light, firing wildly in the air. Women were violated, and innocent children, mothers and the aged were systematically shot. Civilian bodies and their pitiful personal possessions lie scattered through the streets amongst the blackened rubble of this historic town.

Friday, September 4

Have not felt up to writing this week. My influenza has run its course, but it has left me tired and dispirited. My mood has not been helped by the war news. The pins on my map are now south of the Marne River and but a few miles from Paris. We are beaten. All I can hope for now is that Father has somehow escaped this terrible disaster.

The reports place our army, or what is left of it, at Meaux. They have been retreating and fighting for twelve days. What state must they be in? The French have had enormous numbers of soldiers killed, wounded or captured in the battles along their frontiers. The Russian army is destroyed and its generals dead or prisoners.

The war is one month old today. How could I have been so blindly optimistic? This is far worse than anyone imagined. Pessimists talked of a long rather than short war, but even they assumed our eventual victory. Tales of atrocities abound. We shall all be subject to the tyranny of the Hun, no longer the figure of fun in my *Punch* cartoon. I have taken that down.

The Huns seem to have an obsessive fear of terrorists — what they call *franc-tireurs*. In every town or village they overrun, they take hostages, sometimes one from every household, and if there is any trouble, they shoot them. In Andenne, they shot 110 people; in Tamines, 384; in Dinant, 612, including a three-week-old baby.

They are BARBARIANS! And these are the people who are going to win the war! Europe will enter a new dark age.

Saturday, September 5

A note from Anne today. She is unwell and wishes to postpone our picnic. She should not have come to visit me when I was sick. Are we destined never to have this picnic? Will I never kiss her?

Sunday, September 6

In church this morning we prayed for our armies and for their victory. I don't think it will do any good. Missed my walk with Anne. Mother very subdued.

Monday, September 7

The retreat seems to have slowed and even stopped. I have hardly moved some of the pins on my map in several days. Do we have one last chance?

Mother stayed off work today. She remained in bed and, although she allowed me to bring her tea and breakfast, she ate little. She does not appear ill, but she does not talk.

Tuesday, September 8

Mother better today and went to work as usual. She made no mention of yesterday.

The British and French are fighting a huge battle all along the Marne River. Soldiers from Paris were rushed to the Front in taxi-cabs. Will it be another disaster?

ALLIES CROSS THE MARNE RIVER

Wednesday, September 9

HOORAY! Good news at last. The Germans are retreating now. It is nothing less than a miracle. Oddly, on this first day of success, we had rain, the first for weeks. I imagine it will be a relief for our hot and tired soldiers. It is too early to think again of "On to Berlin," but perhaps the tide has turned.

There was a concert in the bandstand at the park this evening. Quite what we needed, some rousing tunes to buck up our spirits. Unfortunately, it appeared to have the opposite effect on Mother, who wept gently all through. I asked what was wrong, but she just shook her head.

I held her hand as we walked home in silence.

Thursday, September 10

The German retreat continues. Iain and I discussed the situation in France. It is a joy to move pins back in the other direction, even if they are not moving very far. Iain says that the Huns' mistake was in sweeping down to the east of Paris. This allowed the soldiers who were brought from Paris (in those taxi-cabs) to attack his flank and force a retreat. If our armies can only get around to the north of the Germans, the way will be open back into Belgium.

Iain is talking of joining up. It is going to be a long slog after all. Kitchener is asking for half a million volunteers to form a New Army. Iain will be of age a year before me and, with his height, he could easily pass for nineteen now. From what Hugh McLean said, no one would question it. What would I do if he joins up? I doubt if I could stand it. It is one thing to have Hugh McLean and Albert Tomkins go, but Iain! Could I join up? Mother would be dead against it, and Anne would be very angry. Did I make a promise to her?

Iain says the three Glasgow battalions have been attached to the Highland Light Infantry, Father's regiment. The 15th is the Glasgow Tramways. They say that a thousand men subscribed in just sixteen hours. The 16th is made up of men who, as children, were in the Glasgow Boys' Brigade. The 17th is the Glasgow Commercials, tradesmen and men of business. Apparently, the 16th has a company of volunteers from Paisley. The Paisley Buddies, they call themselves. I imagine that is where Hugh and Albert are.

Iain is obviously thinking very hard about this. He does not want to go without me, but does not like the idea of waiting until I am old enough. He has agreed to wait a while, but for how long?

Friday, September 11

Anne sent a note today. She is well but feels we should again postpone the picnic as the weather is not expected to improve. I suppose she is right. She says she will see me after church on Sunday.

School begins on Monday. How do they expect us to concern ourselves with sums and the dry dates of English kings when we could be in action?

I came in from the rain this evening with muddy shoes. Mother flew off the handle and shouted that I was a terrible burden to her and caused all the extra work she had to do. It was so unfair. I hardly know her anymore. Some days she is her old self, but others, she is downcast and silent, or angry about nothing. It is very difficult.

The Germans are still retreating slowly. It is nothing like the rush back that our army took after Mons, but it is something. No word from Father. I suppose he has little time for writing. I hope he is all right.

Saturday, September 12

Terrible storm tonight. The lightning illuminates the street brighter than day, and the thunder is constant. The rain is lashing down. It is just as well we cancelled the picnic. It is nonetheless a great disappointment. I bet it is not raining on that lake north of Toronto.

Iain came round today. He said he saw Albert Tomkins in the street. Apparently, Albert didn't tell his mother he had joined up; he just left with Hugh for the Highland Light Infantry training camp down by Largs. When Mrs. Tomkins found out, she was furious. She is a large, strong, ruddy-faced woman, the opposite of Albert, and she is not one to put up with anything she considers to be "nonsense." She got straight on the train and turned up outside the camp, shouting and waving Albert's birth certificate. They had to let Albert go once she proved he had lied about his age. I almost felt sorry for him, being taken back home by the ear. She surely gave him a terrible beating, but that would not have hurt as much as what I imagine Hugh McLean said.

Mother polished the silver again this evening but appears cheerful enough. We certainly have the cleanest dinner service in Paisley.

GERMAN BUSINESSES SACKED

In dozens of outpourings of patriotic zeal, German businesses have been attacked up and down the country. Windows and doors have been broken and some buildings set alight. While such actions cannot be condoned in peacetime, our nation is in the midst of a struggle for its very existence, and any measures to help win that struggle are acceptable. The crowds' enthusiasm was fuelled by the uncovering of several recent cases of spying.

Sunday, September 13

Walked with Anne in a short dry spell after church. Anne brought up the subject of the war.

"Do you see now that it will be long and wasteful?" she asked.

"Long, yes," I replied. "Now that Paris is saved, the war might go on for several months. Maybe even a year. But it is not wasteful. Casualties have been heavier than expected, but France and Belgium were attacked! Were we to stand by and watch the Huns march through the Arc de Triomphe?"

"Please, Jim. Don't call them Huns. They are Germans, yes, but people too. Our butcher has lived on our street as long as I have. He has always been friendly and popular, giving credit, adding scraps for the dog and being generous with his measures. Suddenly no one goes to his shop, his family are shunned in the street, and yesterday some lout threw a brick through his front window. He hasn't changed, but his surname is Schmidt. And the situation will only get worse. Whoever wins, we will never get over all the hatred."

"The war with Napoleon lasted for years and there was no great legacy of hate," I answered.

Anne stopped walking and faced me. "Wellington and Napoleon fought battles with a few thousand soldiers. They were done in a day and there was a winner and a loser. In this war, millions of men are fighting battles that last weeks. Tens of thousands of families are refugees, with no home to return to —"

"Because of the Germans," I interrupted.

"No," said Anne, "because of the war. Yes, the Germans are brutal, but a French or British shell will destroy a home as thoroughly as a German one. I am afraid this war will go on forever —"

"That's nonsense," I interrupted again. "No one *wants* war."

"But, Jim, you're wrong. Lots of people want war. Generals want it. Kings and emperors want it. People who make guns and uniforms and boots and food want it. Even people who sell newspapers want it."

"But what about brave little Belgium?" I asked.

"Perhaps Belgium is just an excuse. Perhaps the war is really about empires and power."

My mind was a turmoil. These were her father's socialist ideas. But they had to be wrong. Surely the world wasn't that complex and devious.

"Even if what you say is true," I began hesitantly, "we still had to protect Belgium."

Anne sighed. "Perhaps. Perhaps all the mistakes were made long ago. But that is no reason to go to our deaths smiling."

"Iain is thinking of joining up," I said.

Anne looked hard at me. "You're not, are you?"

"I'm too young," I replied, avoiding a direct answer.

"Ha," Anne snorted indignantly. "Boys of fourteen are going, I hear. There is nothing to stop you going, too."

"Except you," I said, looking Anne in the eyes. She stared back as if trying to read my mind.

"You mean, if I said it was all right with me, you'd go?" she asked slowly.

After a moment's thought, I responded. "No. A month ago, I was desperate to go in case I missed the adventure. Now I think the adventure will wait for me. It will take a long time to train Kitchener's New Army. Three hundred thousand joined up in August, and there will probably be as many in September. They will all have to be given uniforms, weapons and training. It will be next spring or summer before they will be ready. If the war is still going on then, they and others will be needed desperately.

"I am not as impatient as I was. I wouldn't go without Iain, and I'd have to convince Mother to let me go. There would be no point in joining up if she dragged me back from training camp like Albert's mother did.

"But none of that would matter if you said you didn't want me to go."

I felt the colour rush into my cheeks. Then Anne's hand was on my shoulder.

She kissed me.

It was so unexpected and so quick that I could hardly believe it had happened, but it did. Anne and I have kissed on the lips.

I was horribly flustered and tried to stutter something, but Anne just shushed me.

"Thank you for saying that," she said. "When you really feel it is time, you must go. I'll not stop you. I will not be happy about it and I'll worry myself sick, but I will not hold you against your will. That would only build resentment against me."

So we have kissed and Anne has said she will let me join up. Oddly, I feel less like going now. But I am happy!

September 12, 1914
On the River Aisne

Dear Jimmy,

I am sorry I have not been able to write sooner, but we have all been a bit busy of late. You would not believe some of the things I have seen and done. It has all been a bit of a slog really, not at all like the great cavalry charges we imagined. I have changed my clothes only once in three weeks and, as you can imagine, do not smell too good. But then no one else does, so it does not matter.

I am bunked in an old railway carriage, writing this by the poor light of a flickering oil lantern and the flashes of lightning from the storm outside. It is not the most comfortable billet, but at least I am dry and sheltered. My companions are asleep and I shall be soon, but I have been feeling bad about not writing, and God knows when I will get another chance. I know you will have been following our progress, backwards and forwards, so I will just give you the barest sketch of what we have done.

Our first battle was at a town called Mons, just three weeks ago. We were all keen as mustard. Our equipment and rifles had been endlessly cleaned, and we were raring to have a go at the enemy. The countryside was black and dirty, a mining area, and we were dug in along the canal. We were in makeshift trenches, only about three feet deep, but they were enough cover to kneel in, and we didn't expect to be there long. We were pretty excited and ready for anything. Our two machine guns were set up, and each man was confident he could match or beat the battalion standard of fifteen rounds of rapid fire per rifle per minute.

Just after lunch we started to get some shells coming over, shrapnel mostly, and it made us keep our heads down. One shrapnel ball went through my knapsack, but only one man was wounded. When the shelling stopped, we heard a bugle call and, on looking up, saw the most tremendous sight. It looked like the entire German army was there in front of us, in the open. Jimmy, you wouldn't believe it, wave after wave in their grey uniforms, walking over the fields as if they were on an afternoon stroll. We knocked them down like ninepins, and would have done so again the next day, but the French on our right retreated, and we had to as well or be surrounded.

It was a hard retreat. Day and night, with only stops to fight. Either it was boiling hot and so dusty you felt you were suffocating, or it was nighttime and dark as Hades. On the 26th, we stopped at Le Cateau, warning the enemy not to come too close because the Expeditionary Force still has a sting in its tail. Then it was back to the marching. Word was that we were to be pulled out altogether. The generals thought that the French were beaten and didn't want us to go down with them. But we just kept marching, nearly all the way back to Paris.

My body was screaming for rest. One day, the man next to me actually fell asleep while marching. I wouldn't have believed it possible, but there he was, eyes closed, fast asleep as he plodded along. He even started dreaming and talking about home, before I nudged him and he came to, all startled.

We crossed the Oise and the Aisne and the

Marne, but on September 5 we stopped. I don't think we could have gone on much farther, but I suppose the Germans were just as tired, because they stopped pushing us so hard. We washed and changed our clothes and were ready to go at it again.

The French have been fighting heavily on our right and we have been moving forward slowly as the Germans have pulled back. It is certainly easier to march when you are going forwards.

Now we have returned to the Aisne and are to attack across it tomorrow and, as the orders say, "act vigorously against the retreating enemy." I have an unpleasant suspicion that we will not find a retreating enemy tomorrow. The river is in a deep valley and most of the bridges are down, so it is a natural place for him to stop and fight. But perhaps the French are doing better than us and will outflank him.

Well, I must try to get a few hours' kip, if I can, with this storm and the guns. It has been raining for four days now. At first it was a blessed relief from the heat and dust, but now it has turned everything to mud and it is a complete nuisance.

The storm is really quite something. The thunder is crashing louder than any of our artillery barrages, and the lightning flashes brighten the landscape like noon.

I have not managed to get your helmet yet, though I have seen plenty. Perhaps tomorrow.

I will leave this letter for the cooks to mail and will write again as soon as I can. How is your mother? Look after her and give her my love. Tell her I will write her a proper letter as soon as I can.

Love to you both,

Father

Monday, September 14

At last, a letter from Father! Imagine, while I was listening to that storm on Saturday night, he was listening to the very same one on the banks of the Aisne. It makes me feel so close to him. Iain too was enthralled. He has no one to write to him from the Front.

Mother read the letter with a glum face, and there were tears in her eyes by the end. I asked her why she was crying when Father is all right and in fine health, but she just shook her head and sobbed.

I said, "Don't worry, I'm not going to join up yet." I was trying to comfort her, but she looked at me in horror and fled to her room. I don't understand women. Perhaps I will ask Anne when next I see her — Sunday, if not before. I do wish she went to my school.

First day back at school today. Hugh is the only one missing from my year (Albert is very subdued), but there are many gaps in the years above. The sixth form is talking about joining up *en masse*. I think it was inspired by the assembly address this morning. The rector is from South Africa and fought in the Zulu wars. He told us a stirring tale of the infantry square at the battle of Ulundi and how the British machine guns broke up the screaming hordes of charging Zulus. He said that was the way our soldiers had to break up the Germans, forming squares and remaining steadfast. "Steadfast" is his favourite word and, according to him, is the great advantage the British infantryman has over the troops of every other nation on Earth.

It was an exciting speech, but afterwards Iain pointed out that the Germans are not Zulus — they have machine guns, too.

Very little work was done today, as much of the talk was about the war. It is, after all, the great event of our lives.

Tuesday, September 15

I don't know how I am going to survive an entire school year! Today we studied the early Roman Empire and its wars with Carthage. Normally I would enjoy this, but a voice in my head asked again and again, "Why does this matter?" History is being written by Father and his comrades on the battlefields of France, not in my history class.

Mother appears much better today. She was cheerful this evening, and we sat by the fire and talked as we have not done for many weeks — although nothing of the war. I think I was more worried about Mother's strange behaviour than I have been prepared to admit, even to myself. But there is no sobbing coming from her bedroom, and I shall sleep well.

Infantry Record Office

Glasgow Station

15th September, 19 _14_

Madam,

It is my painful duty to inform you that a report has this day been received from the War Office notifying the death of (N°.) ___G/1513___

(Rank) ___2nd Lieutenant___

(Name) _William Peter Hay_

(Regiment) _2nd Battalion Highland Light Infantry_

which occurred at ___the River Aisne___ on the

___thirteenth day___ of ___September, 1914___,

and I am to express to you the sympathy and regret of the Army Council at your loss. The cause of death was ___Killed in Action___.

Any further information and any articles of private property will be forwarded to you as they are received.

I am

___Madam___

Your obedient Servant

G. Wilson, Major

Officer in charge of Records

Thursday, September 17

It is lunchtime and I barely have the strength to write, but I will try to set down what happened.

Around ten minutes past six yesterday evening, I was sitting by the front window when a policeman came up our walk. Not knowing the reason for his visit, I rushed to open the door. His demeanour and tone of voice told me that something was wrong, but I did not suspect what.

"Is your mother home, son?" he asked.

"Yes," came a choked response from Mother, who had come up behind me. The policeman handed over an official letter, mumbled, "Sorry ma'am" and left.

Mother walked slowly back to the kitchen. She sat down at the table and gazed at the envelope for the longest time.

"Aren't you going to open it?" I asked.

"I wish I didn't have to," she replied. Then, with what appeared to be a great effort of will, she slid a knife along the top seam and took out a single sheet of paper. She didn't cry or scream, but as she read, tears fell onto the page.

"What is it?" I asked, in my last moment of blissful ignorance. It was as if Mother were carved in stone, staring at the letter, tears pouring down her cheeks. I took the letter from her hands. She didn't resist. The words are burned into my soul.

I remember shouting, "No! It's a mistake. It has to be. Father wrote to me just the other day. He was fine. He was going to get me a helmet."

Mother didn't move.

I ran to my room and wept.

Hours later, I found Mother sitting as I had left her. She had not moved a muscle. Her hands were still in front of her as if the dreadful letter was still there.

"Mother," I said, approaching slowly, "you should go to bed."

She did not move. I placed my hand on her shoulder. There was no reaction. I remember talking to her but cannot recall what I said. In any case, it had no effect. At length, I put my arms around her to get her to stand. It was almost as if she had no will of her own but was compliant if the will were supplied.

Gently I led her to her room, where I laid her down on her bed. I made some tea, but she ignored it.

Eventually, I went to my room and slept, fully clothed, on top of my bedclothes. My night was haunted by the most terrible dreams, and I awoke to a dark emptiness this morning.

I went to Mother's room, hoping against hope that she would be better, but she was on the bed exactly as I had left her, staring at the ceiling with unfocused eyes. She did not respond to my voice, nor did she drink the tea or eat the breakfast I prepared.

I am sad, angry and confused all at once. What am I to do?

Writing things down seems to help — at least it stops the tears for a while. Father is dead, gone. He will never tell me stories or play cricket in the park again. I cannot write more.

DOMINION TROOPS EAGER FOR THE FIGHT

Mass recruiting rallies in Toronto's Exhibition Grounds and across Canada have been met with wild enthusiasm by our colonial friends. Thousands are flocking to the colours, eager to do their bit for the mother country. Their chief concern is that they will not be over here in time to take part in the noble cause.

Thursday, September 17, evening

Iain visited after school to see why I had been absent. I poured everything out to him. He was sympathetic, but what could he do? Mother responds as little to him as to me. His only suggestion was that he get Anne; perhaps she could think of something.

When Anne came round, she gave me a hug that should have sent me into ecstasy. As it was, I could barely respond.

Anne had no better luck than Iain and I at rousing Mother. Eventually, Anne made us all some supper, although I did not feel hungry. She then wrote a note to the doctor and delivered it. Unfortunately, the doctor was not in.

Anne had to leave, but Iain offered to stay with Mother and me. I refused. Why should he spend all his time with us? In any case, the doctor would be round soon. Or so I thought.

After Iain and Anne left, I returned to my room to write in my diary and await the doctor. No sooner had I sat down than I heard Mother moving about. I rushed through to the kitchen, thinking the crisis over, but it was not.

The unfocused gaze had not left her eyes. When I talked to her, she ignored me, and if I stood before her, she merely stepped around me. I could take her arm and lead her somewhere, but the moment I released her, she returned to her task — laying out all the silver on the kitchen table and polishing it. She worked silently and systematically, beginning with the knives, moving on to the forks, the spoons and finally the serving plates. When she finished, she began again, cleaning each piece in the same order. To my question, "Why are you cleaning the silver?" Mother answered unvaryingly, "The silver must be kept clean, you know, Jim. Father wouldn't like to come home to dirty silver."

But Father's not coming home. I'm scared.

Friday, September 18

Each day gets worse.

I am exhausted. I did not sleep last night. The doctor did not come yesterday evening, and I spent the night listening to the terrible sound of Mother in the kitchen. She also did not sleep, but remained at the table polishing, polishing, polishing. I feared I would go insane.

Is Mother insane?

The doctor finally came round this morning and pronounced Mother's illness to be "a hysterical reaction" to the news of Father's death. He suggested that the best thing would be to admit Mother to the Alexandria Hospital, where they have a ward for this type of case. I knew what he meant. The asylum ward. I did not want Mother to go there, but she could not remain here, endlessly polishing. I could not get her to eat or drink. At least there she will be cared for and, as the doctor said, hysteria does not usually last long. USUALLY?

Anne arrived while the doctor was here. She did not go to school today as she was worried about Mother and me. We discussed the possibilities, with Mother in the background polishing, and finally decided that the Alexandria was indeed the only alternative. The doctor called a carriage, Anne packed a few things for Mother and I fretted.

A terribly kind nurse took Mother into the hospital and settled her in a bed. Mother refuses to lie down, but sits, gazing ahead, moving her hands as if still polishing the silver. The ward is not a happy place. One woman continually walks the aisle between the beds, asking everyone if they have seen her child. But the room is light and airy and, as Anne pointed out, Mother seems unaware of her surroundings.

Anne brought me home — it is so dark, so empty. She will come back tomorrow. I feel as if I am betraying Mother. But what else can I do? When will this nightmare end?

Saturday, September 19

Spent much of the day with Mother. The nurse said she slept a little last night. Her gaze is still empty and her hands still polish the non-existent silver, but at least she is lying down. Anne went to the hospital with me. She has been a great comfort and help. What would I do without her? All we can do is wait. But what if Mother does not improve?

Sunday, September 20

Another day of waiting at the hospital. Anne's father came with her. He was most solicitous, promising to do anything necessary to help, but Mother remains the same.

Monday, September 21

No change. I have moved into Anne's house. They have a spare room, and I could not continue alone. It is a dream to be close to Anne in the midst of this night-mare. Spent the day at the hospital. I cannot face school.

Tuesday, September 22

Mother the same. Anne is being wonderful, as is her father. I have always thought him a bit odd with his socialist views, but he is truly very kind — and not in the conventional ways of kindness that one might expect in these circumstances. His way is to talk about something completely unrelated to Mother's illness and take our minds off the worry. Sometimes it works. This evening he told us stories of Canada. Anne was too young to remember much, so we both sat enthralled, transported for a short while to a different world — of wide open spaces, and mountains and forests, of skating on the river in winter and canoeing in the summer. It seems a magic place.

Anne's father also has the habit of reading a poem after supper. I know little of poetry, being aware only of Mr. Kipling's verse, Sam McGee and the like. Today we were treated to a new poem published only yesterday in the *Times*. I had never heard of the poet, a Mr. Binyon, but then neither had Anne nor her father.

The poem was about the war, but not the drums and battles. I think of it as talking about Father, and I have cut it out to keep. It is called "For the Fallen," and I find the middle verses comforting:

They went with songs to the battle, they were young,
  Straight of limb, true of eye, steady and aglow.
They were staunch to the end against odds uncounted:
  They fell with their faces to the foe.

They shall grow not old, as we that are left grow old:
  Age shall not weary them, nor the years condemn.
At the going down of the sun and in the morning
  We will remember them.

They mingle not with their laughing comrades again;
  They sit no more at familiar tables of home;
They have no lot in our labour of the day-time;
  They sleep beyond England's foam.

Wednesday, September 23

Mother died last night. The nurse said she just slipped away, moments before Anne and I arrived. Mother looked so peaceful. Her eyes were closed and her hands had finally ceased their polishing. Everyone is being so kind. I feel strangely calm.

Friday, September 25

Mother's funeral. The last few days have been a blur. I am a different person than I was but a few weeks ago. I have lost Father and Mother. I am alone.

September 14, 1914

France

Dear Madam

Please excuse this letter from a stranger, but I am writing to express my deepest regret at the sad loss of your husband, Lieutenant William Hay. It is my hope that the news I can give will be a comfort to you in your grief.

On September 13 last, my company was a part of the Highland Light Infantry attack across the River Aisne. Our first attacks were thrown back by heavy enemy fire. Throughout it all, Lieutenant Hay exerted himself to the fullest and was a credit to his comrades and his unit.

By midday, we were back in our rough trenches, being shelled, and there were a number of casualties lying in the open. One man was delirious and calling for his wife. Although the rifle fire was heavy, Lieutenant Hay crawled out to help him and began dragging him back. But the movement attracted attention and the man was hit again and killed.

Lieutenant Hay was also hit in the chest, but fell back into the trench. There was little his men could do for him. He remained conscious and cheerful until he died peacefully an hour or so later. His last words were for you and Jimmy.

Lieutenant Hay will be sorely missed. Please rest assured that he performed his duty with the utmost gallantry.

Yours in Sympathy,
Arthur Roberts
Captain

Saturday, September 26

Strange, but I felt more emotion reading of Father's last hours in a letter from a complete stranger than I have all this week. Is something wrong with me? I have not been able to cry for my mother. Perhaps insanity runs in the family. All Mother's odd behaviour long before we heard of Father's death. And her hysterics that Father told me of. It must all have been insanity. I am ashamed and scared. Anne told me it was all perfectly natural, but her kindness does not really help. I will have this hanging over me my whole life.

I showed Captain Roberts' letter to Iain. He read it through twice and went very quiet. Then he said that he had decided to go to the recruiting office on Monday morning. He has waited this long because of Mother's illness. What am I to do? I think back on Father's words — almost his last to me — about only fools and fanatics rushing off to war.

Sunday, September 27

I have decided — fool or fanatic, I am going to sign up with Iain tomorrow. What is there to stop me now? Only Anne, and she has given her permission. I cannot stay here. I will join Father's regiment and take his place.

I have reread this diary and find it difficult to believe my childish entries of only a few weeks ago. I am ashamed of my schoolboy enthusiasm, but I will keep this book. Perhaps I shall even write in it again one day, but for now I must concentrate on other things. Tomorrow I will be a soldier.

October 11, 1914
Gailes Camp, Ayrshire

Dear Anne,

Just a note to let you know that Iain and I have arrived safely. No uniforms or rifles yet, but we have 1000 bars of soap, so we shall be clean. We are in F Company, Glasgow Boys' Brigade Battalion (officially, the 2nd City Battalion, 16th Highland Light Infantry), about 200 lads, mostly from Paisley. Hugh is here also. Was he ever surprised to see us!

Will write when I can.

Best regards from your dear friend,
Jim

THE EMPIRE RALLIES ROUND
DOMINION TROOPS SET UP CAMP ON SALISBURY PLAIN

Nothing like the Canadian contingent has been landed in this country since the times of William the Conqueror.

February 7, 1915
Salisbury Plain

Dearest Anne,

It never stops raining. We endlessly march, dig trenches, fire our rifles, line up for dinner, and all in this interminable rain. Everything and everybody is covered in mud and frequently half-submerged. I don't mean to croak, but it does get one down after a while.

Some Canadians are camped down the road from us, close to Stonehenge. I walked over this morning and met an interesting chap, Arthur Hewitt. He hails from Gravenhurst, north of Toronto, in the midst of the lakes where we will have our picnic one day. I think he thought me a trifle odd when I asked him if Gravenhurst was a good place for a picnic! Nonetheless, we got on well. I hope I shall see him again.

The Canadians are an outspoken bunch, not shy of complaining vociferously about the weather, their equipment (they have a remarkable shovel with a hole in it that is supposed to do double duty as a shield but is good for nothing at all) and the local food. They are all excited, as last Wednesday they were reviewed by the

King, a sure sign that they will be going overseas soon.

For our part, we are progressing as soldiers. Our platoon commander is Lieutenant Thorpe, an Englishman, but he does well despite that handicap. He seems like a decent sort and takes his ribbing in good spirit for the most part.

Thorpe is no one's idea of a soldier. He is slightly built with fine, delicate features and an otherworldly aspect to his character that makes Iain and me wonder how he would manage if actually faced with a towering, bayonet-wielding German soldier. He dabbles in poetry and can often be seen off by himself scribbling industriously. When not writing, he reads, carrying a pocket edition of the poet Keats wherever he goes. He came upon me the other day reading the book you kindly sent for Christmas. I did not hear him approach and was surprised by his soft voice saying, "So you are a literary soldier, young Hay."

I jumped to my feet and saluted, but he waved me back down.

"Do you read any poetry?" he continued with a smile.

"Kipling, sir," I said, "and Robert Service's poetical tales from the Klondike."

His smile grew wider. "Never Keats, Wordsworth or Tennyson?"

"At school, sir, but —"

"But you were not particularly fond of them?" he interrupted, squatting beside me.

"No," I said, relaxing a little. "Daffodils and nightingales."

"That is more a problem with the schools than with the poets. Keats's 'The Eve of St. Agnes' has quite a different voice. And there are some modern poets who, I suspect, will have something worthwhile to say about this war we find ourselves in."

"Like Mr. Binyon's 'For the Fallen,' sir?" I asked.

"So you have read some, then?" he said cheerfully. "Mr. Binyon's poem is fine enough, but I was thinking of work that may be created by soldiers themselves."

"But soldiers do not write poetry, sir."

Lieutenant Thorpe laughed out loud. "Perhaps not, lad, but poets may become soldiers. Poetry is all about emotion and experience, and there is no more *intense emotional experience than war. The tragedy of this war may produce some greatness. I feel certain there are some for whose poetic spirit this war will act as a trigger. Perhaps even my own poor scratchings might be of some account. In any case, do not give up merely because some dull schoolmaster had not the wit to see the beauty in a poet's voice."*

"Yes, sir," I said, not quite sure what I was agreeing to. Mr. Thorpe sauntered away, leaving me a little confused. Perhaps I shall try some poets. There is certainly little else to do with our spare time.

What do you think of the letters appearing in the Daily Sketch *and the* Mirror *from soldiers who fraternized with the Germans on Christmas Day? It is hard to believe it was more than a few isolated incidents, and the stories of football matches amongst the shell holes must be exaggerated. The Christmas spirit is all very well, but this sort of thing can only weaken everyone's resolve.*

We all hope for leave soon. May I visit? Iain's Aunt Sadie has moved down to Churchmarston in the south of England to stay with her sister while Iain is in the army, so he will probably spend any leave time there.

*Please keep sending your letters and parcels —
they really do brighten up the life down here. Give my regards to your father.*

Your dear friend,

Jim

HUNS USE POISONED GAS ON DOMINION TROOPS
ALGERIAN UNIT BREAKS BUT CANADIANS STAND FIRM DESPITE HEAVY CASUALTIES

Is there no end to the barbarity of the Huns? Late yesterday afternoon, they released poisoned gas, a weapon specifically banned by the Convention of the Hague, on the Allied forces outside Ypres. French Colonial troops took the brunt of the attack and broke, leaving a four-mile gap in the line. Only prompt and courageous action by the neighbouring Canadian units prevented a serious defeat.

September 25, 1915
Wensleydale Camp

Dearest Anne,

*Just a brief note to say we have settled in safely
here in Yorkshire. In addition to the HLI, there are
units from Lancashire, Gloucester, Warwick and
Northumberland. This peaceful countryside has never
seen so many visitors. The local stationmaster, quite a
character, exclaimed as we got off the train that the town
hadn't been as busy since the last visit of the Black
Dyke brass band. The people hereabouts are very
friendly, although they are somewhat difficult to
understand. I believe they feel the same about Hugh.*

*There are more than 10,000 of us here and we
form the new 32 Division. Unfortunately, we do not
yet have 10,000 rifles and in practice must take turns.
There was some near trouble the other day when the
company Sergeant-major, a foul-mouthed drunkard,
neglected to awaken the men, and we missed breakfast
before a full ten hours of rifle drill in freezing rain. To
top the day off, the Company Commander called us all*

a disgrace, a shame to a noble regiment, and confined us to barracks over the weekend. It was terribly unfair, and some of the men wanted to take the matter further, but at length cool heads prevailed. Leave was reinstated but the company was given extra fatigues. I heard Captain Cameron muttering that compromise is not how things should be done in the army.

But we are not the dregs of society that scared the old Duke of Wellington before Waterloo. All classes and professions are here. We are Britain, and we should be treated as such.

Does that sound pompous? It was not meant to be, but there is a feeling that we are special. We have not joined up for pay or glory, but for our country and for what is right. We can do the job if given the chance.

When not firing at targets, we go on interminable marches along narrow, winding country roads, either in the dust and heat or the driving rain. I can now march twenty-five miles a day carrying a full pack. When we send the Germans running, I shall certainly manage to keep up with them.

A year since Mother's funeral. Father and Mother seem so long ago now. It is not that I feel any less towards their memory, but they belong to a world that no longer exists. I suppose we are fighting to restore their world, but for now we must make do.

Must close now. Iain says hello. And, as usual, please pass on my regards to your father.

Thinking of you and missing you,

Jim

GREAT VICTORY AT LOOS

September 25, 1915, will be a date remembered proudly forever in the annals of British arms. Our gallant troops, many from the New Armies and in combat for the first time, have scored a stunning success amongst the mine tips around the Belgian town of Loos. Yesterday, in the face of stiff resistance and despite heavy casualties, our soldiers penetrated the German line to a depth of three miles. A renewal of the offensive today can only bring breakthrough and total success for our armies.

October 29, 1915
Codford St. Mary

Dearest Anne,

Not long now. All the signs are there. Active
Service Casualty Forms have been issued, the signal
officer is collecting rolls of barbed wire and the transport
officer leaves before dawn every day, returning with
wagons loaded with supplies. All this tells the old
hands that we will be shipping to France shortly. We
are all so excited. The bad news from the Battle of
Loos had us down for a while — the casualties were
so high and the gains so meagre. News of the failure
spread a glum silence through our barracks until
someone shouted, "Are we downhearted?" The instant,
resounding response was "No!" The thought that we
are to get our turn has lifted everyone's spirits.

We will not be sorry to leave this place. We are
camped too close to the horses. The smell does not
bother me, but it does encourage the flies, which are an
awful nuisance. Rats are also common, for the same
reason. They are not such an annoyance as the flies,

although some men, Hugh amongst them, organize hunting expeditions. However, success is not easy, as rats are very intelligent animals.

Iain just ran in to say that notice of leave beginning November 10 has just been posted. Another sign that we will be shipping out soon. A WHOLE WEEK'S LEAVE! Perhaps we will have our picnic?

I will write again soonest.

Your dear, dear friend,

Jim

NURSE CAVELL MURDERED

Nurse Edith Cavell, who courageously refused to abandon her patients when the German hordes swept through Belgium, has been executed by a military firing squad. For the past year, Nurse Cavell has bravely treated the wounded of both sides; yet this is how she is repaid for her courage. In a statement, German military authorities claim that Miss Cavell had been aiding the escape of Allied soldiers.

Tuesday, November 23, on board ship in the English Channel

Dearest Anne:

May I write this diary to you? It was you who persuaded me to take up my pen again and we are sweethearts now, are we not? If I write this to you, I feel that we are closer than the miles between us suggest.

I won't be able to write every day. Even if I did, it would probably bore you to tears. I'll jot down my impressions and thoughts whenever I can. We usually get the *Daily Mail* or the *Mirror*, only a day or two old. No *Glasgow Herald*, but I think I will continue my habit of including snippets that strike me as interesting.

Not that I am writing this for posterity. I see us, in our dotage, great-grandchildren squabbling at our feet and eagerly shouting, "Tell us a story about the war, Great-Grandpa." As I begin, you will groan and say, "Oh no, Jim, not the war again."

We are not allowed to keep diaries in the front lines, but I shall try to carry mine at all other times. Of course, I shall still write proper letters to you when the opportunity presents.

The week before we sailed was one of the happiest in my life. I would say the happiest if it wasn't for the weather denying us our picnic! Nonetheless, the hours we spent walking and talking will stay with me whatever happens over here.

Did we really talk of marriage after this is over? Yes! And of a farm on the vast Canadian prairies, where we will grow wheat and raise cattle and I will become a cowboy just like in the dime novels — Six Gun Jim, the Paisley Kid.

But enough nonsense.

The Channel crossing is quite calm — as Hugh says, "No' as rough as a trip doon the wa'er tae Rothsay." Nonetheless, some of the men are looking a bit queasy. I think the cramped quarters and the overwhelming smell wafting up from the horses below decks are the causes as much as the gentle swell we are riding. We are part of quite a convoy, six transport vessels shepherded by twelve destroyers. It is a sight to see us all, like so many demented zebras in our zigzag black-and-white camouflage with the dark smoke streaming behind as we cut through the grey water. I stood at the aft rail and watched our wake lengthen. A line stretching back to England — to you.

The journey down from Codford was pleasant, with the station platforms lined with cheering people and Boy Scouts who filled our water bottles for us at the stops. We sang and cheered back. It is such a thrill to be on our way at last.

We even stopped for ten minutes or so at Churchmarston, and Aunt Sadie came to see us. Iain is so fond of Aunt Sadie. She brought tea to us on the platform and gave both Iain and me small gifts — hand-knitted socks, mitts and balaclavas — and a pen each, so we can "give her all the news." I am using the pen now.

It was all so sweet that I felt a lump in my throat. Where is my family?

As we left, Iain hugged his aunt and said, "Goodbye, Auntie Sadie." Some soldiers nearby heard this and took up the cry, "Goodbye, Auntie Sadie." Soon the entire battalion was shouting, "Goodbye, Auntie Sadie. Good old Auntie Sadie!" Iain was mortified, but she seemed quite chuffed at all the attention. She really is splendid.

In contrast, it was a small, grim scene at Folkestone as we were waiting to board. There was a hospital ship docked alongside, and the wounded were disembarking. Some were on stretchers, but many, with arms in slings or heads bandaged, made their own way down the gangplanks. We were all keen to see them, as they had come from the Front and we wanted to see if it is true that men who have recently been in battle have a different look to their eyes.

I should have thought the wounded would have been happy to be home for a well-deserved rest, but they just looked tired and downcast. Most shambled along with heads down, faces yellowish and ghostlike, eyes surrounded by bags of skin and cheeks hanging limply. Only their eyes darted about, not resting on any one thing very long.

One man I found particularly disturbing. He passed close by me and our eyes met. His were a deep grey, but they had a haunted, distant look. We were only a few feet apart, yet he did not see me. His focus was on something far more distant than the physical world around him. What horrors was he seeing? Frightening as his face was, I recognized that faraway look — it was Mother's look in the asylum. Will I look like Mother and this poor soldier after I have been in battle?

There was a strange silence hanging over these men, almost as if speech was not worth the effort. Cheery words died on our lips.

As the wounded passed, a man from their ranks broke the silence with "Are we downhearted?" We responded with an ear-splitting "No!" He snarled, "Well, you bloody well should be." It quite took us aback. Men with such a cynical attitude have no place in our forces.

Well, I must finish now, as we are approaching Boulogne. In a short while, I shall be standing on French soil. I have read and thought about the country so much, I feel I know it, but I am sure it will have a few surprises for me.

CANADA PROMISES BRITAIN 20 MILLION BUSHELS OF WHEAT

Wednesday, November 24, in camp, Boulogne

We did not arrive in camp until late last night, after a long hard slog through the town and up the hill. A steady rain turned to flurries of wet snow, making our march unpleasant. Still, a few locals came to cheer us on. I would have thought they would have seen enough soldiers by now.

On disembarking yesterday, some of the men, in their eagerness, ran down the gangplank. A corporal in the Royal Scots was lounging against a dock bollard.

"Hey!" he shouted. "You dinnae want tae run in this country."

"How no?" Hugh asked.

"Weel," the corporal replied, "you get paid, you get fed, you get bedded, whithir you run or no'. An' when you get tae the Front, you'll no' be wantin' tae run awa, fer twa reasons. Wan, it's safer tae stay where you are, and twa, if they catch you, they'll shoot you. So the only time left tae run is at the Germans and it wid be an auffy stupid man who runs tae get intae a battle."

His attitude was not to be commended, but we are now learning to mimic the casual, measured walk of the veterans we see about us.

The camp is on a hill dominated by a large radio tower. It is a tent city paved with duckboards and surrounded by a high barbed-wire fence, through which the local ragamuffins gaze and make faces. The place has an air of seedy permanence, although we shall be here only a day or two. I do not think we will even have an opportunity to visit the town. We could as easily be back in our camp on Salisbury Plain.

Saturday, November 27, a barn near Surcamps

The last two days have been amongst the longest of my life. We marched out of camp on Friday at three o'clock in the morning — too early even for the pipers to play us out. By five-thirty, we were at the station. The railway carriages bore the inscription "Hommes 40, Chevaux 8," and there was much discussion — did this mean 40 men *or* 8 horses or 40 men *and* 8 horses? If the latter, which end of the horse would it be best to stand at? Fortunately, we humans had the carriage to ourselves.

Even so, we were packed in like pilchards. At first we were in good spirits and cheered at the short halts, but as the morning wore on, the halts became longer and the cheering less enthusiastic. At length we were stopping, in the middle of nowhere, for no apparent reason, for a half hour at a time. At some halts we even climbed down to boil water for tea and to cook bacon.

That night we were more exhausted than after a twenty-mile route march. And we had to do it all again today. But at least we are here now. The rest of the way is on foot.

We are billeted in farms around this town, the men in barns, the officers in the farmhouses. I don't know which is better, since each house has a large manure pile by the door. The old woman at our farm claims her's dates back to 1870. Apparently, family valuables are commonly hidden in the centre of the manure pile in times of trouble. It would take a very determined thief to go looking for them.

Sunday, November 28, a farmyard in France

We did not march until noon today in order to have a church parade this morning. The chaplain (Charlie he is called, after the comedian who is so popular now and who we saw in *Mabel at the Wheel* that afternoon) is a pleasant man, not fire and brimstone, which would not go down well with the lads, but easygoing enough to accommodate all. He writes letters home for the men who cannot write. He has organized the men with the best voices into a choir and has a portable harmonium to drown out the rest of us on the psalms. This morning, he preached a short sermon (his brevity also makes him popular) about loyalty and duty, and then gave a drumhead communion to those who wished it.

After church, we marched fifteen miles, and most of us thought back fondly to the train. We each carried a full pack, 120 rounds of ammunition, iron rations (these are emergency rations — bully beef, tea, sugar and biscuits) and rifles — a heavy load, especially on these French roads. We were glad to reach this farm, even though there was not enough room in the barn for us all. Many of us are making do in the open. Fortunately, it is not raining, and we are warm around the fire we have made from a nearby tree sacrificed for the war effort.

CHINA ASKED TO JOIN ALLIES
TRULY A WORLD WAR

Monday, November 29, another nameless farm

At first light, we were awakened by a small man wearing a bowler hat and a tricolour sash over his suit. He stood, red-faced, at the edge of the farmyard and berated us angrily in very fast French. The interpreter (the interrupter, in the slang) was awakened, and the verbal stream was aimed at him.

Apparently, the little man is mayor of the local village and the tree we cut down and burned last night is a local landmark, "the finest apple tree in all of Picardy," by his account. He demanded compensation to the princely tune of 100 francs, about 5 pounds. That is more than three months' pay for me, and I suspect he could purchase much of an orchard for that. He was eventually taken into the farmhouse to meet the commanding officer and left an hour or so later considerably mollified.

A hard day of marching. The only consolation is cool weather. This would be hard indeed under a summer sun. We march for an hour, then rest for ten minutes. The countryside is quite pleasant, with small woods and villages joined by tree-lined roads, which are extraordinarily straight. From a distance the land appears flat, but it consists of long hills that sap our strength.

Villages are often the worst, as the streets in them, and for a mile or two before and after, are cobbled with large blocks of stone, none too carefully laid. This makes the ground uneven, and the studs on our boots slide on the smooth stone as if it were ice.

Each village is built around an open square and dominated by a church. The locals come out to see us pass and, despite the curses we mumble at every slip on the cobbles, we always put on a show, roaring out a song to the accompaniment of the pipes. The villages seem populated almost exclusively by old men and women, although I suspect girls are there but kept indoors. In one village, a girl appeared in a doorway and was greeted with a chorus of shouts and whistles. She was hurriedly hustled out of sight.

Tuesday, November 30, Bertangles

St. Andrew's Day. A pleasant billet, which we are sharing with some Indian soldiers, tall, proud men in turbans. It is strange to see them in this setting, so far from home, but they seem cheerful enough.

When we stopped marching this evening, we launched into our usual routine of billeting and preparing for the night, but this evening it was different. Iain and I were laying out bedding in the barn and chattering when Iain touched my arm. I noticed that the other men had fallen silent. I thought perhaps an officer had arrived on a surprise inspection, but then I heard a dull rumble in the distance.

"Thunder," I said. "It is as well we are under a roof tonight." But Iain shook his head. Then I realized — it was the guns we were hearing. Although we are miles away from the Front, the noise of the cannonade can carry to us. It reminded us all that we are not here on a holiday hike. There is some serious work to do soon.

GANDHI RETURNS TO INDIA CALLS FOR PEACE

Wednesday, December 1, Pierregot

The guns are continuous now and cannot be far off. Iain says the particularly loud ones are probably the fifteen-inch naval guns. We can actually feel the ground shake. Yet there is no major action occurring, just the normal activity of this war.

We are to stay here for several days. To learn the routine, each company will be fed into the line for a couple of days at a time. I am of two minds about it. On the one hand, it is what we are here for and I am still as keen as ever. On the other hand, I have a perfectly normal fear of the unknown. I suppose it is the quelling of that fear that will make a true soldier of me.

KITCHENER'S ARMIES RARING TO HAVE A GO

Tens of thousands of young men, who a little more than a year ago were carefree clerks, shopkeepers and tradesmen with little concern other than who was going to win the big match on Saturday, are being shipped over to France for their first taste of life in the trenches and their first Christmas away from home.

Wednesday, December 8, Pierregot

So much has happened in the last week. On Sunday night, F Company moved up to the line at a place called Thiepval Wood. We replaced the Seaforth Highlanders and had red tabs sewn on our sleeves to distinguish us. We marched up in the dark, through a nightmarish world of chaos and blackness, lit only by flames flickering from ruined buildings, the flashes of guns we passed and the occasional flare soaring through the sky. Close to the Front, there is the inescapable smell of ashes.

The closer we got, the more jumbled everything became. Piles of equipment lay, apparently haphazardly, beside the road. The buildings began to show damage, at first just the occasional hole in the roof, but later entire walls missing. At one crossroads, two poor horses had been caught by the explosion of a large shell. They lay, still hitched to the remains of the limber they had been pulling, in the middle of the road. We had to make a detour around them. I tried not to look at their bloated bodies, but could not help but notice that the skin around their mouths was drawn back in a hideous mockery of a smile, exposing long yellow teeth. What was worse was the smell. The pungent odour of decay mixed with the ordinary smell of horses, such a common odour of home that its juxtaposition with death turned my stomach. Why had the poor beasts not been decently buried?

After what seemed like forever, we descended on wooden duckboards into a communication trench. This we followed for a considerable distance until we reached the section of front line that was to be our responsibility for the next few days. With the hand-over formalities complete, a company of Seaforths squeezed past us to get to their well-earned rest before daylight.

As it was almost dawn when we were settled, there was no opportunity for sleep. In the lines, we must stand to every day before sunrise because this is the favourite time for an attack. As the sun came up, the first thing that struck me was how messy everything was. In our practice trenches in training, we were severely disciplined if anything was left lying about. Here, old equipment hangs everywhere, and all manner of makeshift utensils and periscopes litter the dugouts and trench walls.

The trenches are only about four feet wide and eight deep. The wall facing the enemy, the parapet, is lined with sandbags and has a fire-step that enables men to stand up and shoot at any attackers. The back wall, or parados, is supported by a network of entwined branches, revetting it is called. Every few yards, the trench dog-legs at ninety degrees to minimize the blast effect of any shell or bomb that might land in it.

The officers have reasonably roomy and secure accommodation dug deep into the trench sides, but the men must make do on the fire-step or in small individual dugouts, funk holes they are called, carved into the wall — and if you are lucky — with an old piece of tarpaulin draped over the opening to keep out the rain. Everything is wet. Even when it is not raining, dampness oozes out of the ground. And everything smells, a sort of rich earthiness with undertones of sweetness. It is not unpleasant, and I began not to notice it after a while.

The daily routine in the front line is simple. We are up before dawn to stand to arms in case of attack. With the first light, rifles are cleaned and inspected, a tot of rum is given out (foul stuff that burns the throat — I give mine to Hugh and his friends, who seem to thrive on it), then breakfast and usually back to the funk holes for more sleep until dinner at noon. In the afternoon, there are three hours or so of work repairing damage to the trench, watching the enemy through the periscopes and doing odd jobs, such as digging new toilets. We stand to again at dusk, the time of most activity. At night we work. Even if we have time off, it is impossible to sleep for the noise. In the dark, most men are busy, either laying or repairing wire in front of the trench, bringing up supplies from the rear or digging listening posts out under no man's land. Working at the listening posts is the most frightening, but also the most interesting. In them, you feel very exposed and alone. It is sometimes possible to hear the enemy talk — a reminder that he is also out in no man's land listening to you.

The first morning in the lines, Iain and I were examining our new surroundings. To the left of F Company, our line runs around the front of Thiepval Wood and down into the valley. Facing the wood on the high ground of the ridge is the village of Thiepval, dominated by the ruins of a large chateau that the Germans have turned into a formidable strong point. To our right, the line swings around in a salient called the Nap. It faces another German strong point christened the Leipzig Redoubt. Straight ahead of us, across gently sloping open fields, the German lines sit in front of yet another strong point, the Wonderworks we call it.

I was waxing on about how well designed our trenches were as Iain was scanning through a wooden periscope, the only way to see above the parapet without exposing yourself to enemy snipers.

"I don't think so," he said.

"What do you mean?" I asked.

"Well," he said, "they are built well enough, but look at our location." I peered through the periscope at the world above. The grass-covered ground sloped gently up to the German trenches some 250 yards away.

"Now look back," Iain ordered.

The view was remarkably similar, although the ground was more scarred with trench lines and shell holes.

"What do you see?"

"I don't know." I was unsure of what Iain was getting at.

"The ground slopes up on both sides of us," he said. "That means anyone attacking the Germans will have to charge uphill, while the Germans can charge downhill. Also, any water will drain into our trenches. Why do we not dig them behind us on the hill? They would be drier and more comfortable, and we wouldn't have the enemy looking down on us."

What Iain said made sense, but there had to be something we were missing. Surely the generals wouldn't put us in a bad position for no good reason.

"I'm sure there is a reason," I said rather weakly.

"Perhaps," Iain replied, but he didn't seem convinced.

"There is a reason."

We both jumped. Lieutenant Thorpe was standing behind us. Instinctively, we straightened to attention.

"Stand easy," he said. "The reason is that we are here only temporarily."

As Mr. Thorpe seemed disinclined to continue, Iain asked, "I beg your pardon, sir? Temporarily?"

"The High Command regards trenches as a temporary stopping place before the attack is renewed. If they are too well-sited defensively or too comfortable, the soldiers will be less inclined to leave them to attack."

"But, sir," Iain responded, "these trenches have been here for more than a year. That is hardly temporary."

"Just so," Mr. Thorpe replied. Then he looked more intently at me. "Young Hay. Still reading?"

"Yes, sir," I replied, as Iain stared at me.

"It has not been a good war for literature. Brooke and Grenfell gone. And now Stadler."

"Stadler?" I queried.

"Ernst Stadler," Thorpe elaborated. "A very fine poet."

"His name sounds German," Iain said.

"Yes," Mr. Thorpe replied. "I met Ernst at Oxford. He studied and taught all over Europe — Canada, too, I believe. He was killed outside Ypres. The Germans produce poets too, you know.

"Have you read Keats yet?" he asked me.

"No, sir," I said, a bit ashamed.

"Oh well, no matter. Perhaps you will one day." Then he reached into his pocket and produced a creased page torn from *Punch*. "You might enjoy this. It is published anonymously, but the word is that the author is Canadian. Carry on."

Lieutenant Thorpe saluted roughly and wandered off down the trench. Iain and I looked at each other curiously.

"What was all that about?" Iain asked.

"Oh, he found me reading that book that Anne sent for Christmas last year and has got the idea that I am some kind of literary intellectual, so whenever he sees me, he talks about poetry."

"He's an odd bird, all right."

The page Mr. Thorpe had given me had a poem on it — "In Flanders Fields" by Anonymous. At first I thought it was going to be another depressing piece about the dead, but Iain and I both liked the image of the lark flying above the guns, and the call to take up the "quarrel with the foe" was rousing. I wonder why the author doesn't want his name known? If I ever write anything, I'll want my name on it.

Living in the trenches is remarkably safe as long as you remember to keep your head down. Shelling is not a problem unless one lands exactly in the trench, which very rarely happens. A shell landing a few feet away will make a loud noise, but all the blast will pass over the top.

A greater danger is the continuous sniping. The Germans are very good at letting fly just at the top of the parapet, so anything sticking up is in danger. That is how we had our first casualty in the battalion. Last week, a man in A Company (oddly, man number 1 of Section 1, first Platoon, of the first company) was shot in the head and killed. He was careless, but I don't know why we don't have tin helmets to help stop such waste.

We came back out of the line this morning — just two days to give us a taste. It was quite an experience, although rather boring considering we were so close to the enemy. There was only one unpleasant moment.

Last night, while we were awaiting relief by C Company, I was on sentry duty. This entails crawling along a sap dug out into no man's land, standing, listening, watching and trying to keep warm and awake. The previous nights had been bitterly cold with hard frost, but last night the temperature rose and we had heavy rain. The ground was slick, and there were several inches of mud and water in the bottom of the trench. I became thoroughly wet and covered with heavy mud. The wait was cold and unpleasant, but I was also scared. In the darkness, every little noise, even a rat scurrying past, was magnified by my imagination into hordes of Prussians storming towards lonely me.

The trench wall in front of where I sat had partly fallen — a shell had landed nearby the previous day. This gave the wall an irregular outline, which my mind kept resolving into attacking soldiers. My imagination ran riot, and once or twice I was on the verge of firing away at nothing. I was sweating, despite the coolness of the night.

My agony was ended by Iain escorting a member of C Company to relieve me. I did not tell him of my fear and quickly retreated down the reserve trench.

The normal routine will be six days in reserve, six days in the front line, six days in rest, then back to reserve again. There will be a big attack with the New Armies, but not before spring, when the weather improves. Then we will show them what we can do.

So, Anne, I am a real soldier now, not exactly battle-hardened, but I have been in the trenches. I will write you a proper letter tomorrow. Good night.

Is that silly? To say good night, I mean? You won't read these words before we have both had many more nights' sleep. I just felt the urge to write as if I were talking to you, even though you cannot reply. I miss you, but I must to sleep now before I become maudlin.

POET KILLED

The promising young poet Charles Hamilton Sorely has been killed in action near Loos. Although not of the stature or temperament of Brooke, he showed great promise for someone only twenty years old. His best-known work is "When You See Millions of the Mouthless Dead."

Thursday, December 9, Pierregot

Quiet day cleaning up and resting. We are far enough away from the Front that only the largest shells can reach us, and they are very infrequent. Despite that, the landscape is heavily brutalized from the soldiers' occupation, equipment and horses. We live in tents, often of our own devising. We shamelessly scrounge — it is never called stealing — anything to make our situation more comfortable. Still, the cold seeps through our thickest clothes. Many times each day, I fervently thank Aunt Sadie for her generous gift of woollens. The artillerymen, of whom there are many this far back from the line, often wear heavy goat or sheepskin jackets, which, despite a strong animal smell when wet, are highly prized.

Friday, December 10, Pierregot

Again a quiet day. Iain is organizing a football game against the 17th HLI on Sunday. Our team was good in training camp — let's see if we can continue our dominance in France.

It is an odd thing, Anne, but on the days when I have the most time to write, I have the least to say. Despite our being within range of the enemy's guns in the greatest war in history, life, for the most part, is unutterably boring. One day is much like the next — parades, marching, carrying and resting. The only things that stand out are the entertainments. A dozen men from F Company dressed as women and dancing around on a makeshift stage with sheets for curtains is considered an artistic triumph here.

This is a very changed war from the one that Father fought so briefly. He marched for weeks, but we sit in trenches that have not moved for a year. The strain of our position merely induces a lethargy and unwillingness to undertake anything out of the ordinary. In addition, I find that writing reminds me of home and makes the situation here even less enjoyable.

I have decided, therefore, to write only when I have something to say. If my daily round is dull, that is no reason to make my diary dull (else what will succeeding generations think!). So, until I feel the creative spark, adieu.

TOWNSHEND BOTTLED UP AT KUT

In the Mesopotamian campaign, Major-General Charles Townshend and more than 8,000 British troops have taken refuge from the Turkish forces in the desert town of Kut-el-Amara. This is a sad end to Townshend's attempt to capture Baghdad. However, relief is a mere twenty miles away on the Tigris River and the siege is not expected to last long.

Sunday, December 12, Pierregot

Already something to write about. We played the 17th this afternoon and trounced them soundly. Your soldier hero, despite the handicap of playing right back, scored the winning goal, his first. I was forward for a corner kick. The ball swung in and landed at my feet. Almost before I knew what I had done, I'd hit it past their keeper, who was at least as astonished as I. That gave us a two-goal-to-one lead, from which we never looked back. Iain, who plays beside me at left back, joked after the game that he would lose me to a forward position and that after the war I had a great future with St. Mirren, or maybe even Celtic or Rangers. Even Hugh, who expresses his aggressive nature as sweeper, the last line of defence in front of our goalkeeper, congratulated me afterwards. I must be careful that my head does not swell so much I fall over with its weight.

AUSTRALIAN AND NEW ZEALAND TROOPS EVACUATED FROM SUVLA BEACHHEAD

Over the last few nights, the entire ANZAC force holding the beachhead at Suvla Bay on the Gallipoli Peninsula has been evacuated. This extraordinary feat has been accomplished without a single casualty. Unfortunately, they leave many comrades buried amongst the rugged hills and gullies. Only British troops now remain at Cape Helles.

Sunday, December 19, reserve trench

We moved up here on rotation the Monday night after my famous football game. Six days carrying equipment about, laying duckboards and wire and doing other tiny tasks, the sum of which must be our war effort.

Life in reserve is fairly safe, although we are within range of many types of artillery and even long-range machine-gun fire. There are a couple of places that are noted danger spots — one especially cannot be safely passed in daylight. The enemy have artillery zeroed in on road junctions and such, and they lob the odd shell. We quickly learned these spots, ducking low and hurrying through them on our errands.

Tonight we go in for our stint in the line, which means we shall be there over Christmas. We have all been told many times that there is to be no celebrating like last year. Any non-belligerent contact with the enemy will be dealt with most severely, so it looks as if the chances of us all leaving the trenches spontaneously and coming home are slim.

In any case, I will wish you and my diary a Merry Christmas and will write of my adventures when I return to rest on Boxing Day.

CONFIDENTIAL

This year there will be no repetition of the unauthorized fraternization that occurred last Christmas. The artillery is to maintain a slow rate of fire throughout the day, and every opportunity must be taken to inflict maximum casualties upon any of the enemy who appears in the open.

Boxing Day, Pierregot

MERRY CHRISTMAS! Today is my favourite day of the season, but for different reasons this year. A quiet spell in the line, probably because of the bitter cold snap that has us all struggling to keep warm. One man on sentry duty even had to be taken out of the line for frostbitten fingers. He was the only casualty in our company. Apart from the occasional shell and some desultory sniping, our lives were bearable.

Our orders to remain in our trenches yesterday were obeyed, unlike a year ago, when, the veterans tell us, soldiers of both sides left their trenches to bury the dead and fraternize.

Although there was no football this year, there was an unspoken Christmas Day truce along the Front. Very little firing could be heard anywhere. For one day, at least, it was live and let live. Around three o'clock yesterday, we were called to stand to as the sentries reported increased activity in the German trenches. We all stood on the fire-step awaiting whatever devilish trick the enemy had planned for us. At length, something rose from the enemy trenches, but it was not hordes of grey-clad attackers. It was a large sign, elaborately decorated with paintings of trees and sleighs and the words "MERRY CHRISTMAS, JOCKS."

The regiment across from us is from south Germany, Saxons, I believe, who are more inclined to let things be than the Prussians from the north. Our lads laughed and shouted back, "Merry Christmas to you too, Fritz."

There was some considerable banter, and a few men even attempted to lob over cans of bully beef in exchange for German sausage, but the distance was too great. Around dusk, the Germans began singing, hymns mostly, ending with "Silent Night." It was quite moving, and we all listened in silence. When they had finished, a voice called over in English, "It is your turn to give us a song now, Jock." As not enough of us knew a suitable hymn, we gave them a collection of soldiers songs. "Tipperary," of course, and several others. We ended with "Mary Had a Little Lamb," all eleven verses, only one of which was suitable to be sung by children.

The Saxons seemed well pleased, and we settled down to our festive dinner, not up to the standard of home or even the one supplied by the kind folk around our camp last year, but pleasant nonetheless. Most men had some small treats from home, which were shared out. We did very nicely, thank you.

The whole occasion was very emotional, and some became quite maudlin on the extra rum ration. It is odd to think that the trenches on the other side are filled with men trying to stay warm and dry, just as we are. I wonder if a young Saxon soldier is writing a diary to his sweetheart? It is usually easy to think of the enemy as "them" — inhuman monsters intent on our death and destruction. But it is difficult when you have joked and sung songs with them! Are these men who wished us Merry Christmas the same ones who butchered women and children in Louvain and Dinant? Perhaps soldiers in the trenches are all the same. Maybe, if it were left to all of us, we would pack up and head for home. But after ten steps, we would, Saxon and Briton alike, be arrested and shot for desertion. So we remain.

My favourite day of the year was made even better when I came out of the line this morning to find your parcel waiting for me. I have put the comforter, socks and gloves to immediate use, as Aunt Sadie's are the worse for wear. The chocolate and cake will be impressed into service soon, as will the book. I have not read any stories by John Buchan, but this one looks diverting. I assume the thirty-nine steps of the title are a part of the mystery. Great literature is all very well, but a good adventure takes one's mind off the trials here.

Well, I will sleep now, because even in a quiet time in the line, there is precious little opportunity. Re-reading this, it seems like a letter rather than a diary entry. I miss you. Good night.

DOUGLAS HAIG TO REPLACE SIR JOHN FRENCH AS COMMANDER-IN-CHIEF OF THE BRITISH TROOPS ON THE CONTINENT

After our disappointing showings at Neuve Chapelle, Ypres and Loos this past year, much is expected for the new year under the new commander. Haig will have Kitchener's soldiers at his command and can be counted upon to use them to good effect. The Hun had better look out come the spring weather.

Friday, December 31, Pierregot

Another year, and still the war goes on. It will certainly be over by Christmas — but which Christmas?

Last year almost everyone went out celebrating, and I was the exception for staying behind. This year Hugh and his cronies were the exception for going to the local *estaminet* to drink the old year out. Many men sat alone and pensive. Iain and I talked of the war.

"Next year will see an end to it," I began.

"That's what we all said last New Year." Iain is becoming quite cynical.

"But 1916 will be different," I said. "The New Armies are ready, and once the spring weather comes, the Big Push will see us through the German lines and on our way over open country."

Iain shook his head. "I see two problems with that. First, you saw the fortifications the Germans have at places like Thiepval and the Wonderworks —"

"Our artillery will take care of those," I interrupted.

"Perhaps," Iain went on patiently, "but the Germans are nothing if not thorough. I imagine they have dug very deep dugouts, where they will be safe. I doubt if they regard their trenches as merely temporary."

I opened my mouth to object, but Iain hurried on. "I am not saying it's impossible. If we are trained to go around the strong points while the artillery is forcing the Germans to stay in their dugouts, we might make it through to your open ground and leave places like the Wonderworks for mopping up later."

"If that's the way to do it," I said, "then I'm sure that is what the generals have planned. It will be plain sailing."

"Even if it is, there is the second problem," Iain explained. "Say we get into open country past the German front lines. We can advance only as fast as we can walk — and must stop often to allow the artillery to catch up. The Germans will have plenty of time to organize another front line a few miles back, and we will just have to start all over again."

"The cavalry!" I exclaimed. "Once the lines are breached, they will rush through and create havoc. That's what they're for."

"What they *were* for," said Iain sadly. "Today, the Germans will not even need a trench system to stop cavalry. Half a dozen machine guns could easily destroy a regiment of the finest horses. The days of cavalry are over."

"You're too negative," I said loudly. I was angry, but I couldn't think of a good argument against what Iain was saying. "If you think it is all so impossible, why are you here?"

"I don't think it's impossible," he replied calmly. "I just think it will be very difficult. It will require clever organization by our staff officers and might take longer than this coming year. Now let's not argue. There is enough fighting without that."

"All right," I agreed. "Let's hope I am right and you are wrong."

Iain is being pessimistic. Next year *will* see an end. I hope.

No. This year. Here we are in 1916. Happy New Year — the year of victory and of our picnic.

Friday, January 7, 1916, in reserve

Into the line tomorrow. We are becoming quite familiar with the routine. Weather remains cold and activity down. I think soldiers on both sides are mainly concerned with keeping warm.

I have finished Buchan's book and enjoyed it very much. Iain has it now but will wait until we return to read it, as the chance of losing or damaging things in the front line is too great and the book too precious. I have a small volume of Keats that I shall take with me in order to fulfil Lieutenant Thorpe's reading recommendation. Oddly, I found the book abandoned in a basement in which we were billeted last week. It is water damaged and missing a few pages, but most is readable and I shall not mind too much if it is lost. The book has already caused me some grief. Hugh happened to be with me when I found it. "Is tha' a book o' pictures o' they French ma'moiselles?" he asked.

When I said no, that it was poetry, he laughed and became quite nasty, asking why I should want to read "tha' nancy rhymin' stuff." Thanks to Hugh, I am now getting a reputation as a sissy. I don't mind too much — there are more important things to be concerned with here. Wish me luck.

LAST ALLIED TROOPS QUIT GALLIPOLI

After suffering some 252,000 casualties in the nine-month campaign, the last British troops have been removed from the battlefield at Cape Helles.

Friday, January 14, Pierregot

Back after another stint in the front line. We are all beginning to feel like old hands. Three trips to the Front and, except for those frostbitten hands (the man's own fault), no casualties in F Company yet. I imagine that, as the weather improves, we will be more active and the risks will increase. Word is that we are to be moved north for some rifle and bombing training. It will at least be a break and a chance to see a different part of France — although I rather like this area around the Somme River. Such rolling country must look very pretty in the summer.

The vista is dominated by the church spire at Albert. The town is behind the Front but changed hands early in the war. It has not been heavily shelled, but the church, which is used for observation, has been hit. The church spire is crowned with a huge golden statue of the Virgin Mary that now hangs out over the street below. The belief is that the war will end when the Virgin falls. She certainly looks very precarious. I suspect our engineers have been busy with rope and wire helping her defy gravity. Will she fall this year?

I read Keats's poems and, although the language is a bit flowery for my taste, I must admit that I enjoyed some very much — the imagery is vivid. As Lieutenant Thorpe predicted, I particularly enjoyed "The Eve of St. Agnes," but perhaps that is just the images of cold and frost that seemed so apt as we shivered at stand-to every morning. I was also taken with Keats's description of statues as "sculptur'd dead," although it is not accurate. The dead are more like rag dolls than statues.

On our first morning in the line, I looked out through a periscope aimed at one of the few remaining trees standing between the trenches. Imagine my shock when I realized there was a soldier sitting amongst the bare branches. I jumped backwards, almost knocking Hugh over.

"Hey!" he shouted angrily. "Watch whit yer daein'."

"There's a soldier in the tree," I said. "It's an attack." Hugh pushed me aside and looked through the periscope. He burst out laughing.

"Aye," he said when he had calmed down a bit. "It's a sojer a'right, but he'll no be daein' ony attacking."

I looked again. The man, or what was left of him, was a German soldier, all right, but he had been dead a few days. I imagine he had been caught by a shell on a night patrol and flung into the tree. He hung limply, twisted in an unnatural position, as if there were no bones in his body. Mercifully, his helmet obscured his face.

"Better make sure though," Hugh said, aiming his rifle through a firing slit in the sandbags.

"There's a spy up in yon tree!" Hugh shouted, loosing off a round. Soon several men were firing away at the corpse, letting out yells of glee whenever a jerk of the body signified a hit. The Germans retaliated, and in no time bullets were flying above our heads.

This went on until Lieutenant Thorpe appeared and put a stop to it. The firing gradually died away on both sides.

It was horrible, Anne. I have had some black dreams about it. We are becoming less than human, just as you said we would, the day we saw Hugh with the rat down by the mill. I didn't shoot, but I did watch all of it through the periscope. My pulse quickened as each shot hit home. What is becoming of us?

SIX DIE IN CANADIAN PARLIAMENT FIRE

Six men died as the beautiful mock-Gothic central tower of the Canadian Parliament buildings in Ottawa collapsed. The library was saved.

Thursday, February 10, in reserve

Is it really almost a month since I last wrote? Time flashes by in repetitions of the mundane, but it also drags interminably, as we appear no closer to going into battle. Yesterday, however, we came within an ace of seeing real action, and that has galvanized me to write.

We stood-to all day yesterday. Apparently the Germans had occupied a section of our trenches opposite the Leipzig Redoubt, and we were to take it back. It was unnerving waiting with all our battle gear, ready to do what we had signed up to do, yet scared of the danger. In the end, the King's Own Yorkshire Light Infantry retook the trench without our help, but they suffered some sixty casualties. If those casualties had been ours, who would they have been?

We have been issued gas helmets, large blue flannel affairs, very cumbersome and suffocating, although I suspect we shall not mind, if we need them.

Our headquarters are at a town called Bouzincourt, about five miles back, beyond all but the largest shells. The town is noted for its teacher, a Monsieur Hie, who has an almost fanatical hatred of Germans. Apparently, before the war, he was famous for having the most beautiful calligraphy in the entire region.

One afternoon a stray shell blew off his arm — the one he did his calligraphy with. Since then, he keeps a German helmet, with a bullet hole in it, on his desk.

How desperately I wanted Father to get me a souvenir helmet. I think I even wanted one with a bullet-hole in it. It all seems so macabre now. Helmets are not toys — they save lives here. Not that we have helmets — it is still cloth caps for us — although there is word that we are to be issued with tin helmets before the Big Push in spring.

DEMONSTRATORS IN BERLIN PROTEST FOOD SHORTAGES

The effectiveness of the naval blockade of Germany has been shown by angry demonstrations in the capital over increased rationing and a shortage of basic foodstuffs. The German will to fight is being seriously undermined.

Friday, February 11, in reserve

We are to miss the next spell in the line for the bombing course. I am pleased not to be going to the Front, not because of the danger, but because the going in and coming out are so dreadful. Everything must be carried in and out of the trenches on men's backs, and we are little better than pack animals.

When I go into the trenches, I first put on almost every piece of clothing I own. From the ground: boots, socks, drawers, puttees, trousers, braces, vest, shirt, cardigan, waistcoat, jacket and cap. At times it is difficult to move freely, but warmth is crucial. Over this bloated form are strung, suspended and strapped: pouches, haversacks and belts containing or supporting field dressings, waterproof sheet, blanket, gas helmet, mess tin, rifle, bayonet, entrenching tool, water bottle, 150 rounds of ammunition, soap, toothbrush, spare socks, drawers, shirt, towel, greatcoat, iron rations, knife, fork and spoon.

In addition, we will soon have the long-promised tin helmets (not that we will complain at those), and often there is extra equipment, such as wire, duckboards, sandbags, food and water. It is sometimes difficult enough to stand, let alone walk all night through winding, cramped trenches.

The grind of the work and the monotony of the endless daily routine are much harder to bear than any danger, which appears minimal unless one is careless or unlucky. We are all frightfully keen for the spring attack to come so that we can get on with what we came for.

For now, we will have to make do with the course for a change of pace. We set off tomorrow for Étaples on the Channel coast.

MAJOR GERMAN OFFENSIVE LAUNCHED AGAINST FRENCH AT VERDUN

Seven German army corps, almost 300,000 men supported by massed artillery, have opened a devastating attack on the French forts around the crucial town of Verdun. Although suffering high casualties, the French *poilus* are bravely resisting this first assault by the Hun since the Ypres attacks of last year.

Saturday, February 26, Mailly-Maillet

What a delight to be back in familiar surroundings. I have become almost fond of the peaceful Somme valley. Away from the trenches, you would hardly know there is a war going on. Of course, there are soldiers, horses, mules and transport everywhere, but the countryside is quiet and the farmers go about their work as if nothing were amiss.

The Front, that thin line, only a few hundred yards wide, running from Belgium to Switzerland, is a different world. It is a vast machine, a grinder into which nations thrust men from all corners of their empires, and out of which those men return changed, if they return at all. Yet, simply walk a mile or two and you are back in the real world. It is possible to think this way only when one is out of the trenches. While at the Front, it seems the most natural place to be — far better than Étaples, at least.

Étaples is a dreadful place and I shall die happy if I never see it again. It is a vast camp with thousands of soldiers. The centre is a huge training area, called the Bull-ring. Most days we were there it was covered with a thin skim of snow.

Every day we were roused at 5:45 for a meagre breakfast of porridge. At 7:00 we went to the Bull-ring, and there we stayed, in all weather, until 5:30 each evening. There was the familiar bayonet training and pointless marching, but the chief focus was drilling by platoon and unarmed combat. We are now all proficient in doing very serious damage to another human being with our boots, knees and teeth. Apparently, another means will arrive with our helmets — they have a lip around them that can be smashed into an enemy's face.

I know that men are killed in war and that I may be called upon to kill some, but the idea of ripping a man's ear off with my teeth or smashing his nose to a pulp with my head is loathsome. I hope it never comes to that.

We are camped, back on the Somme, in a wood by this rather pleasant little village. On Monday we move back into the line before Thiepval, but we have an easy day tomorrow. Of course, there will be divine service and many small tasks to perform, but it will be as close to rest as we manage in this war.

We share the village with a battalion of Ulstermen from the 9th Royal Irish Rifles. They are not in good spirits, as one of their number has been court-martialled for desertion and is to be shot. The Irish feel that this is unfair, and there is some talk of taking matters into their own hands. Groups of disgruntled soldiers can be seen huddled on street corners in the village. Their officers should take them in hand, especially as the Irish are a very volatile people.

I hope we do not become mixed up in this affair. Execution may seem harsh, but army discipline must be maintained, and a firing squad is at least a quick and clean way to die. One man who doesn't do his duty can put many of his comrades at risk.

Étaples made me feel very low at times, and I missed you, Anne, very much. I miss you here too, of course — that will not change until I am back in Paisley, sitting at your dining-room table discussing poetry with you and your father. But, oddly, my spirits have climbed steadily as I move closer to the Front. It is difficult to explain the feeling of being part of some great and worthwhile adventure that we all have. We cannot wait to show the world what the New Armies can do. It will be a while before the Spring Offensive, but we could do no good at Étaples, and this is what made us all feel a bit down.

Well, it is time I was luxuriating in a dry billet. Good night.

Sunday, February 27, Mailly-Maillet

What horror my "day of rest" brought! I can hardly write, but must. We will be in the line tomorrow, and who knows when I will have another chance.

I awoke early, as I had been doing at Étaples. The birds were singing and the sky was lightening to the east. It promised to be a pleasant day, and I decided to begin it early with a stroll in the woods before breakfast. I wish I had not.

It was still dark in the trees, and I almost stumbled over a small knot of soldiers deep in discussion. They stopped talking as soon as I appeared, but I did hear "The boys will not fire on young James."

One of them stepped forward aggressively and asked, "Who are you?"

"Jim Hay," I replied. Then, feeling bolder, "Who are you?"

The soldier looked very rough. He was my height, but broad and obviously very strong. He peered out from under dark bushy eyebrows. I noticed that his nose had been broken at some point and wondered vaguely who had broken it.

"Who I am is none of your business," he snarled in a strong working-class Irish accent. "This is our billet and our doings are no concern of yours."

I was about to retreat when one of the soldier's companions stepped forward. He was taller than the first, but even the weak dawn light showed his face to be friendlier.

117

"Ease off, Allen, he's only a boy. Maybe even younger than our James. What's your unit, lad?"

"F Company, Sixteenth Highland Light Infantry," I said.

"A Kitchener boy," he said. "They moved into the village yesterday. Off to the Front tomorrow. Do you know what's going on here, young Jim Hay?"

"No," I answered.

"One of our friends is to be shot this morning."

"For nothing!" the short one spat.

Feeling emboldened by the tall soldier's presence, I asked, "Is that the soldier who deserted?"

"Deserted?" Allen shoved his face in front of mine. I could smell his foul breath.

"James Crozier is but newly eighteen," he snarled. "He joined up underage in the first month of this damned war. He served all this winter in the trenches. It's this war that's going to be killing him."

"We were at the Redan, before the village of Serre," his companion explained more calmly. "James was on sentry with his best friend. A shell caught them both. I was the first one there. James was slumped against the trench wall with a glazed look, covered in blood. I thought he was badly wounded, but there wasn't a scratch on him — it was all from his mate. I scraped some bits off James and scratched around in the mud, but there wasn't much of his friend left. Must have been a direct hit —"

"A lad bigger than me," Allen interrupted, "and you couldn't find enough of him to fill a haversack. No wonder James went a bit loopy."

"It was the shock, you see," the first soldier explained. "I thought James would be all right, so I got busy trying to clean things up. But when I looked around, he was gone. He tried to ... to walk home. Some silly idea about having to tell his friend's mum and dad what had happened.

"He was picked up two days later and sent to the hospital, still dazed and complaining of pain all over his body."

"Shell-shock if ever I saw it." Allen couldn't seem to keep quiet. "And what did that stupid doctor say? Nothing wrong! He should be under the shells with his friend's brains all over him, instead of sitting safe at some base hospital saying half-crazy boys are fine."

"Anyway," the tall soldier went on, "they court-martialled James. He is to be shot this morning for desertion."

"The firing squad won't do it. They'll refuse to shoot one of their own boys," Allen said.

"Maybe." His mate sounded uncertain. "But they'll just bring in men from outside. At least this way it will be his friends. I think —"

He was interrupted by a loud, angry voice.

"You men! What are you doing over there? Get up on parade at the villa."

The dark shape of an officer loomed between the trees. With scarcely suppressed grumbles, the men began moving up the hill to the edge of the wood.

In the poor light, the officer would not notice that I was from a different unit if I stayed with the others. But if I split off, there would be trouble. I shouldn't have been wandering around the woods, and, with all the trouble, the officer wasn't likely to go easy on me. Slowly, I began moving with the rest of the men.

The tall soldier seemed to understand my dilemma and whispered. "Come be an outside witness to what happens this day."

We marched in loose formation about twenty yards to the rear garden wall of a small villa. As we rounded the wall, I saw the rest of the Irish battalion, 750 men or so, formed up in a loose, open square. Close to the wall was a wooden post. In front of the post were twelve nervous men in two rows.

There was a small hut at the far end of the wall, probably a gardener's hut. A murmur ran through the soldiers as out of the low door stepped a chaplain reading from an open Bible, followed by an officer and three soldiers. The middle soldier was being supported by the other two. I assumed he was James Crozier.

Crozier looked around, stumbling and seeming completely unaware of his situation.

"He's drunk!" I gasped in shock.

"Yes," whispered my companion. "And the drunker he is, the better. They've been feeding him rum all night. Most of the firing squad are the worse for liquor, too."

The tension amongst the watching soldiers was almost a living thing. Even as Crozier's hands were tied behind the post, he seemed oblivious. He was mumbling unintelligibly and looking around vaguely. The sun was creeping over the horizon, shining on his face. His hair was reddish and his nose and cheeks were covered in freckles. The top buttons of his uniform were undone.

Crozier watched with detached interest as the officer pinned a brown envelope over his heart.

"The target," my companion said.

The crowd fell silent as the officer walked back to the firing squad.

"Ready!" he said loudly. The squad shambled to attention, their rifles across their chests.

At the harsh sound of the order, Crozier jerked his head up and with an effort focused on the men before him.

"Aim!" The men brought their rifles to their shoulders. You could have heard a pin drop.

Crozier's eyes widened in horror. At last he understood what was about to happen. "No!" he screamed, struggling against the ropes. The officer appeared to hesitate.

"I don't want to die!" Crozier cried, tears streaming down his cheeks. A spreading dark patch stained his trousers. "I want to go home."

I felt sick, but I couldn't look away.

"Fire!"

A ragged volley followed, mixed with the zing of bullets ricocheting off the wall. The crowd gasped.

Crozier had been hit, but he was still very much alive. He had slumped forward and the rope had slid down the pole so that he was now on his knees. There was a trickle of blood on his left cheek, and he was sobbing quietly.

The officer stepped forward, unbuttoned his holster and pointed his pistol at Crozier's swaying head.

The crash of the single shot was louder than the entire volley. The firing squad had dropped their rifles. One man was on the ground retching.

Blindly, I shoved my way back through the crush of men and towards the trees, but Allen blocked my way.

"That's army justice," he said angrily. "A boy from the shipyards joins up to fight for his country, and look how they treat him. No better than the Germans!"

I pushed past him into the trees.

The weak sun was fully up by the time I stumbled into our billet. Men were drifting over to the mess wagon for breakfast. I was half blind with tears and, with little clear idea of where I was going, I barged my way through the men. I heard Iain call my name, but I ignored him. Eventually, I slumped down against a tree, crying uncontrollably.

As long as I live, I shall never forget the sound of that solitary pistol shot or the look on James Crozier's face when he realized he was about to die. Whatever he had done, he did not deserve that.

As I calmed down, two things stuck in my mind. The army that I was a part of — the army that was fighting this just war — was capable of its own frightful acts. And James Crozier was obviously sick. His glazed look reminded me of my mother and of the shell-shocked soldier I had seen at Folkestone. If I could spot it, why could the army doctor not see it? And if he did see it, how could he claim that Crozier was fit? Perhaps the army had decided to make an example of Crozier to keep his companions in order. If so, it had not worked. Those Irish soldiers were very close to mutiny.

I had calmed down by church parade. Iain looked at me strangely when I arrived for the chaplain's sermon. This afternoon I told him what had happened. I am not sure he fully believed me. He said there must have been more to the situation than I had realized. Perhaps. Only yesterday I thought deserters should be shot. Now ...

We are for the Front tomorrow — I must try to sleep. I hope my dreams are not too bad. Good night, Anne. How I wish I were with you.

GERMANS DECLARE WAR ON MERCHANT SHIPS

Not even neutral ships on the high seas are safe from the spreading tentacles of Hun barbarity. Under the flimsy excuse of being forced into the action by the Allied blockade, Germany has launched a dastardly submarine war against merchant vessels plying their legal trade. Coming on top of the *Lusitania* disaster last year, this decision can only bring President Wilson and the United States closer to joining the crusade.

Friday, March 24, Pierregot

Another month without writing. After poor Crozier's death, I became very low. For several days, all I could do was automatically perform my duties. Iain said it was as if I had been mesmerized. Fortunately, our simple tasks can be carried out without engaging the brain. What my brain was doing was thinking of home. Normally, I do not feel overly homesick, apart from missing you, of course, but my mind dwelt on nothing but images of home, you, Mother, picnics in the sun and, oddly, Iain's Aunt Sadie. I think she is family for me now that I have none. I write to her almost as much as to you.

I have also been plagued by bad dreams. At first they were about Crozier, but a recurring one has us on our picnic. It is a beautiful sunny day and we are sitting by a river. I should be happy, but I have this premonition of doom. You are chatting away happily, your back to the river. All of a sudden, the calm water ripples and a huge black dog breaks the surface — a horrifying beast, with glaring red eyes and slavering jaws. It surges out of the river and bears down upon us. I shout to warn you, but you keep talking and smiling, completely unaware. It is me the beast wants. I try to stand and run, but it is as if I am mired in quicksand. I manage to reach my knees before the hideous creature is upon me. I can hear the animal's harsh breathing, feel the weight of its paws on my chest and smell its foul breath in my face. It is going to tear my throat out. The last thing I see is you, sitting calmly, chatting and nibbling on a dainty sandwich.

What does it mean? I have no idea, but I always wake up soaked in sweat and unable to return to sleep. Fortunately, the frequency of the dream is decreasing. I am now visited by my nocturnal horror only once every week or so.

We have been in and out of the trenches as many times as the others, yet they have suffered men killed, while our only casualty remains the man with frostbitten fingers at the end of last year. It seems we lead a charmed life. Let's hope it is so.

A batch of five newcomers arrived today. They are to replace soldiers who have been drafted out of the company to specialist jobs. Iain and I were filling sandbags when they marched in after dinner. There, as large as life and not ten feet away from me, was Albert Tomkins.

"Hey, Albert!" I shouted.

At the sound of his name, Albert whipped his head round so fast I thought he would strain his neck. He looked positively frightened and scuttled over to us.

"Quiet. Quiet," he hissed urgently. "I'm not Albert."

"Yes, you are," I said. "And this is Iain. Hugh is round behind the barn. We all went to school together before the war. Remember?"

"Of course I do!" Albert was very agitated. "But I'm Tommy now. Tommy Atkins. I joined up under a false name, so Mum couldn't find me and take me home again. You won't tell on me, will you?"

"No," I said. "Your secret is safe with us. Go and grab somewhere to sleep, and say hello to Hugh."

Albert grunted and scuttled off. He had never been that big, but without all the endless marching and drilling that had filled us out, he looked positively scrawny.

"Can you believe that?" I asked.

Iain replied, "I think he is more scared of his mother than of the Germans."

Laughing, we went back to filling sandbags. It was good to see Albert, but how out of place he looked! He was a reminder of a time that had vanished. We are not the boys he remembers.

Saturday, March 25, Pierregot

Another day of "rest," spent loading shells onto the light railway that runs to the ammunition dump outside town. We went to the *estaminet* in town this evening with Hugh, Albert/Tommy and some others. It is remarkable how some civilians have adapted to wartime. The *estaminet* is the living room of a house, run by Madame. She is a woman of very few words, but over numerous visits we have established that she had two sons. One died in the first days of the war in one of the frontier battles that I took such glee in. The second was in the air force and crashed last autumn. Her husband is fighting at the big battle of Verdun.

The two boys, large strapping country lads, are commemorated in black-draped photographs on the mantle. Of the husband there is no sign. Perhaps one has to die to be displayed.

Tables, scavenged from shelled houses, are crammed into the room with just enough space between to allow

Madame to pass. This she does, carrying a huge, heavy jug of *vin blanc* — "vinky blinky" the soldiers call it. She slops the almost-yellow liquid into the odd assortment of glasses held up, retreats to the kitchen, where she refills the jug from some mysterious endless supply, and then parks herself on a rocker by the door, awaiting the next summons. The wine is cheap and barely drinkable, with a harsh, bitter bite. I have not acquired a taste for it, but Hugh and some of the others enjoy it, and their state at the end of the evening attests to its potency.

My sense of unreality at having Albert appear from the seemingly distant past was strengthened this evening. He talked of home, which is becoming increasingly remote. To us it is important to know the flight of a 5.9 from that of a shrapnel shell. It's difficult to get excited about some local politician lining his pockets. (Does that sound like something your father would say, Anne?)

Albert is also very enthusiastic about the war. We are eager as ever for the Big Push this spring, but our simplistic ardour is now tempered with a reality that Albert has yet to experience. We know there is a job to be done and we will do it, but there is little of the shouting and flag waving of a year ago.

Listening to Albert made me realize how much this war is changing us all. Will we change back after it is over, or is this the birth of a new kind of man?

So much for philosophy. It must be the vinky blinky talking.

RUSSIAN OFFENSIVE COLLAPSES

After several days of heavy fighting around Lake Naroch, the Russian offensive, launched to relieve pressure on the French struggling around Verdun, has collapsed. Reports put Russian casualties at more than 100,000 men.

Sunday, March 26, Pierregot

Big football game against the 17th. Iain scored two goals, but we went down four goals to three — a titanic struggle.

We are to go up to the line tonight, before our time and not to our usual spot at Thiepval. Apparently, the French are so hard-pressed at Verdun that they must take troops from wherever they can. We must take over the sections of the Front they vacate.

CORNISH STONE SHIPPED TO FRANCE

Thousands of tons of stone from quarries in Cornwall are being shipped to France to provide bedding material for the hundreds of miles of railway lines being constructed to carry supplies to the Front. Sources of local stone have been exhausted.

Friday, March 31, in reserve

Why must we get so little respite from horror?

We took over a section of French trenches early on Monday morning, to the south of Thiepval. The state of the trenches was a severe disappointment. Sections of the wall were collapsing, and in some places we had to duck or be exposed to sniper fire. Drainage and dugouts were virtually non-existent, and poorly dug toilets seeped back into the trench bottom, enveloping all in a foul smell. There was another odour, too, a vaguely familiar sweetness. Its source became hideously obvious on the second night.

I was digging into the trench to shore it up when my shovel sank unexpectedly deep into the earth. I jerked it back, creating a small avalanche of dirt and a hole, from which emerged the most nauseous smell and the decomposing remains of a human foot and leg. I collapsed, retching helplessly on the foul trench floor.

Hugh was working beside me. "Whit's the matter?" he asked.

All I could do was point helplessly at the horror sticking out of the mud.

"Oh grand," Hugh said with a smile, "that'll mek a grand hook for hangin' ma kit aff."

How can he think such a thing? This wasn't a rat. This was a human being.

I was shaking uncontrollably, unable to take my eyes off the foot.

"Still," Hugh said, stepping forward, "I suppose yon

nancy officer'll no wish to have this clutterin' up his nice tidy trench." With that, Hugh hacked off the leg with his shovel, stuffed it in the hole and pushed the earth back in place. Then, as calm as you please, he returned to work.

I gradually stopped shaking and, keeping well clear of the soft spot in the trench wall, finished our work shift. But I have been plagued by some terrible dreams. Unfortunately, the sweet smell is everywhere — not nearly as strong as when I released it from the hole, but enough that horror overwhelms my tired brain, and I have great difficulty digging anywhere.

Oh, Anne! How I long to be somewhere clean, where the air is fresh and horror is only a thing of storybooks.

I must try to sleep now, although I fear what it will bring.

Monday, April 3, *in reserve*

The dreams have returned. I dread the nights.

However, my daytime mood was helped by your package today. I have just written to thank you, Anne, for the jam, socks, biscuits and wonderful fruit cake. Your cakes are legendary in the company — I always have as many friends as I could wish for when I pick up a parcel from you.

Iain received a parcel from Aunt Sadie. It was not as imposing as my own, but Aunt Sadie must have spent much time and love preparing the homemade dainties.

There was also a letter — one of the nicest I have ever read. I have copied it out below. She is as sharp as a tack and, although she can have no experience of the trenches, reads the casualty lists and between the lines of both the official reports and Iain's censored letters to create a picture of our lives that is, I suspect, closer to reality than many people at home have. We go back to Thiepval tomorrow to resume our regular routine after the bitter spell in the French lines.

March 31, 1916

Churchmarston

My Dearest Nephew,

I sincerely hope this finds you as well as it leaves me.

The enclosed treats will, I trust, brighten what must be a very tedious existence for you boys. Be sure not to hog them all to yourself, but share them with that nice friend of yours, Jim. A more practical gift of some woollies is also on the way, as I am sure it is just as unseasonably cold where you are, and you will not have the luxury of stepping inside to warm yourselves by the fire.

There is beginning to be talk of a big offensive in the spring. I imagine it is true, and I fervently hope that it succeeds in bringing this dreadful conflict to a close. However, it strikes me that, if I am hearing of this in my little village in England, it is more than likely that

the Germans, who are probably efficiently seeking such
information, know about it also. It is possible that they
may be quite well prepared for our offensive. With this
in mind, I urge you and Jim to be as careful as you can.
I know you will do your bit, but I pray nightly for the
safe return of my favourite nephew, as I do for your
young friend and all the other lads who cheered me so
on the railway platform last year.

I must close now and attend to my crocuses and
daffodils. They are late this year on account of the
cold winter.

My love and blessings to you.

Aunt Sadie

Sunday, April 9, Pierregot

Another quiet time in our usual trenches. The dreams
have eased.

This evening was spent in a routine invented spe-
cially for this war — chatting. A small group of men
sit on ration boxes around a tobacco tin lid held over a
lighted candle. We remove our shirts and, with exquisite
care, comb along the seams, capturing the lice that
inhabit that cosy place. When we find one, and it is not
hard as there are many hundreds in each shirt, the little
devil is dropped onto the hot tin, where he pops most
satisfyingly. I suppose it really does no good. There is no

lessening of the itching the next day, but it is strangely relaxing, and much social intercourse is carried on around the candle. Today our activities were doubly useless, as we have just heard that we are to go for a bath and delousing tomorrow. Such is the logic of this war.

Monday, April 10, Pierregot

This morning we all marched down to the old brewery in town — then stood around in the cold, clutching our towels and soap until it was our turn for the baths.

The brewery has to be seen to be believed — although, Anne, you should never cast your ladylike eyes on the goings-on within. About two dozen wooden tubs line the walls, half-filled with lukewarm water. When we enter, we undress and our clothing is taken away to be immersed in foul-smelling disinfectant to discourage its lice population for a few days.

Shivering and pale, the naked men run to the tubs, where they scrub vigorously, as much to restore circulation as to get clean. Then it is out, a quick dry and back into "clean" clothes — never the ones you handed in upon entering. It is primitive, to be sure, but there is little to compare with feeling clean and knowing that I will not be scratching for a few days.

Wednesday, April 12, Pierregot

Back to reserve tomorrow. It is a four-day cycle now, rather than the six-day one of last winter.

VETERAN CORRESPONDENT DIES

Mr. Richard Harding Davis, the veteran war correspondent who first brought news of the atrocity of Louvain to a shocked world, has died of a heart attack. Mr. Davis was 52.

Friday, April 14, in reserve

Loaded shells and filled sandbags. It is repetitive and apparently endless. When will we attack?

Monday, April 17, in reserve

Into the line tomorrow. Let us hope our luck holds.

Saturday, April 22, Pierregot

No one got a scratch. In fact it was the quietest spell we have seen. The Saxons opposite appear to have gone to sleep. Perhaps they have gone home and left only a solitary corporal to lob over the occasional trench mortar or fire off his rifle before breakfast. Would that that were true. Big football game tomorrow. We hope to get our revenge on the 17th.

COASTAL TOWNS SHELLED

Yarmouth and Lowestoft were yesterday shelled by German cruisers. Fortunately, casualties are reported to be light.

Sunday, April 23, Pierregot

And revenge we did get. A trouncing, seven goals to two.
Iain got a hat trick. I had little to do in defence but cheer
on our attack, and they only scored twice at all because
we lost concentration in the last fifteen minutes.

Our victory was marred by their team being
without their two star players, a midfield dynamo and a
short, fair-haired, bandy-legged right winger who,
before the war, was being scouted by Celtic. He could
dance around anyone as if the ball were tied to his right
boot. Both were wounded during their last spell in the
line. The midfielder is only slightly injured, but the
winger has lost a leg.

REBELLION IN DUBLIN

In an apparently coordinated uprising, Irish rebels have
taken over several government buildings, including the post
office, in the heart of Dublin and have fired upon British
troops. This is a particularly treacherous act at a time when
the Empire is fighting for its very life.

Monday, April 24, Pierregot

I cannot help but think of the Irish soldiers I met when
Crozier was shot. To rebel at a time like this, even for
a cause as justified as home rule, is unforgivable. Irish
boys die over here just as easily as the English or Scots.
It is a stab in the back.

ARTILLERY REDUCES LAST IRISH STRONGHOLD

The last of the Irish rebels in the post office on O'Connell Street surrendered this morning after heavy shelling by field artillery units destined for the Western Front. The rebellion is over, but much of Dublin is in ruins and the hatred still festers.

Wednesday, May 10, in reserve

Our luck in front of the Wonderworks is over.

This last spell, we faced a new regiment, very active and not at all like the live-and-let-live Saxons. They were continually firing with rifles, machine guns and trench mortars. Most had little more than a nuisance effect, but yesterday a shell landed in our trench, close to where I was resting. I heard shouts and ran to help.

Two men were lightly wounded, but one, Tom McDonald, was bleeding heavily from the leg. I bound a tourniquet around his thigh and tightened it, despite his protestations that it was causing him considerable pain. At least it slowed the bleeding.

Lieutenant Thorpe radioed in and talked to the medical officer. When he returned, he looked very serious.

"How does it feel?" he asked Tom.

"The tourniquet hurts something fierce, sir," Tom replied.

"I am afraid the MO thinks an artery is severed," Thorpe said. Tom's pale face was creased with pain, but he kept his gaze on Lieutenant Thorpe. "If that is the case, only surgery can repair it."

"And the doctor cannot get here before I bleed to death," Tom finished.

Thorpe nodded slowly.

"Well then," Tom said, turning to me, "perhaps you'd be good enough to fetch me a cigarette and loosen this damned rope around my leg?"

If I released the tourniquet, Tom would be dead in a few minutes. Lieutenant Thorpe nodded again. Then he pulled out his silver cigarette case, placed a cigarette between Tom's lips and lit it. Gently, Mr. Thorpe removed my hand from the knotted rope and loosened it. Blood welled up through the jagged rip in Tom's trouser leg.

"That's much better," he said, sighing.

We sat in silence for what seemed like an age. The blood formed a surprisingly large pool in the trench bottom. Finally, Tom shivered once and closed his eyes.

Not all that long ago my main concern was there being enough wind to fly my kite. Now I have watched men die.

Lieutenant Thorpe said that at least Tom's death was peaceful. This is true, but I doubt if I shall ever forget his sad white face as he left us. He was twenty-two.

That night, Lieutenant Thorpe was ordered to take out a patrol into no man's land to assess the German positions and, if possible, bring back a prisoner for questioning. Iain and I, Hugh and Albert, and four other men blackened our faces and followed Mr. Thorpe over the parapet and through our wire at 2:15 a.m. We left our packs behind, strapped our rifles over our backs and took our bayonets and an assortment of clubs. Hugh's club was a wicked-looking thing covered with bent nails.

It was a cloudy night, and the thick blackness was a comfort as we edged across the stubble and around the scattered shell holes. It was slow going, as we were much more likely to be heard than seen, and we had to lie flat and silent whenever a star shell lit up the landscape. It took us forty-five minutes to cross the 250 yards to the German wire and another half hour to cut a way through. Our object was a forward sap, which would have two or three soldiers in it. We could hear the men talking as we edged closer, and I could see the mound of sandbags just in front of me. I felt as alive as I have ever felt. My only worry was that the enemy would be warned of our approach by my deafening heartbeat.

On a low whistle from Mr. Thorpe, we lunged forward. The Germans were taken utterly by surprise and disarmed before they knew what was happening. One big man put up a bit of a struggle, but a tap from Iain's club and the sight of Mr. Thorpe's revolver soon quieted him. It was strange to see the enemy close up. They looked just like us — one was even a lad my own age. They were scared, but Albert was the one who was fidgeting nervously.

"Which one'll we tek back?" Hugh whispered.

"All three," replied Lieutenant Thorpe. "We cannot leave two to give the alarm."

"Aye we can, sir," Hugh went on, fingering his club.

"We will not kill prisoners," Mr. Thorpe said firmly.

We rummaged around the sap and collected papers, weapons and anything else that might be of use. Then, with Mr. Thorpe ordering the prisoners in whispered German, we climbed out of the sap and retreated through the wire.

All went well until we were about halfway back. A star shell from the German side lit up the landscape. We all flopped down on our bellies, except the big German, who turned and began running back to his line. Hugh made to go after him, but Mr. Thorpe kept him down just as all hell broke loose. Machine guns opened up on both sides, and the escapee staggered and fell before he had gone twenty yards.

I tried to press myself as far into the ground as possible. I could hear Albert whimpering beside me. We were fairly safe as long as we kept flat and waited for the fuss to die down. But this was Albert's first time out. With a terrified screech, he began to get up.

I suppose he was trying to run back to our trenches, but he was still crouched when the bullets hit him. The first group tore into his chest and pushed him upright. The second caught him in the head and spun him around. He was dead before his limp body landed across my back, with what remained of his head close to my right ear. I could feel his warm blood soaking my jacket and running down my neck.

I should have been horrified — and I was shocked, yes — but my overwhelming feeling was relief. With Albert's body on top of me, I was much less likely to be hit. I am not proud of that feeling, and I did feel sorrow and regret for Albert afterwards, but I must honestly tell what I felt at the time. Has this war turned me into a monster?

I twisted my head away from Albert's. To my left was the young German soldier. His face was a white mask of terror. His arms were spread wide, his fingers convulsively digging into the soil. Instinctively, I reached out my arm and held his hand. I smiled and he returned it.

Behind him, I sensed as much as saw two prone bodies locked in an urgent scuffle. By the dying light of the flare, I saw a nailed club rise and fall.

We lay for nearly an hour as flares lit the night. As the gunfire waned, Mr. Thorpe whispered orders. With me bringing Albert's body in and Iain escorting the prisoner, we crawled back through our wire and fell thankfully into our trenches. The young German was passed down the line for interrogation, after which he will be sent to a prisoner-of-war camp. He will be safe back in Britain before I will.

When Lieutenant Thorpe asked if anyone had seen the third German, Hugh smirked.

"Ah saw him, sir," he said. "He tried tae escape, sir."

Hugh waved his club, which had blood and what looked like clumps of hair on it.

"When did he try to escape?"

"Just efter yon big yin got up and ran," Hugh answered. "I didnae want him givin' the alarm, so ah hammered him, sir."

There was almost an insolence in Hugh's attitude.

Thorpe looked hard at Hugh. Then he said, "I hardly think he was about to stand up and run after what had happened to his companion. In any case, giving the alarm was no longer an issue."

Hugh shrugged. It was obvious that Lieutenant Thorpe didn't believe him and he didn't care. Could he have just killed a prisoner in cold blood as easily as he had the rat in Paisley? Only Hugh knew.

"It'll be dawn soon. Go and clean up," Mr. Thorpe ordered.

The next day, we came out of the line.

I am feeling very low. It is difficult to keep enthusiasm up in the face of what I have seen. On top of that, the biggest battle of the war is going on at Verdun, and all we do is short spells in quiet sections of the line and mindless hard labour in reserve. Deaths like Tom McDonald's and Albert's seem such a waste. I know our big attack is coming and that the weather must improve before we can launch it, but the waiting is so hard.

Thursday, May 11, in reserve

Albert was Tommy Atkins in the army's records. I assume he also used a false address. Only Iain, Hugh and I know his real name, but none of us knows his address. Hugh says it was somewhere on Moss Street, but he doesn't remember the number.

Albert's mother must be told the sad news. Hugh does not care — he says it was Albert's stupid fault for standing up — and Iain thinks we should just tell

Lieutenant Thorpe and let him set things to rights. But it does not seem fair that Mrs. Tomkins should get only some impersonal form letter, like the one we received about Father, and then only once the official wheels have ground out Albert's real identity. How would Aunt Sadie cope if that was the way she heard of something happening to Iain? So I wrote to Mrs. Tomkins, care of our school. They will forward it, and she will be able to ensure the army has Albert's grave properly marked.

It was the hardest letter I have ever written, and I destroyed a good many drafts before I finished. I began telling Albert's mother truthfully how her son had died, but the horror of his death appeared senselessly cruel when written to someone who has not seen what our lives are like.

Eventually I ended up with something much weaker than the truth, but probably as much as Mrs. Tomkins can take. I merely said Albert had been killed on a raid, but didn't say how, and told her he helped capture the prisoners. I said Albert died quickly, which was true, and cleanly, which was not, but perhaps the bigger lie was suggesting that there was some point to his death. I try to justify my lying with the hope that it will make Mrs. Tomkins feel a little better.

I had just finished when I felt someone behind me. Seeing Lieutenant Thorpe, I jumped to my feet.

"Well, my literary friend," he said, "letters make a change from your diary. Who is the lucky recipient?"

Taken by surprise, I blurted out, "Albert's mother, sir." Mr. Thorpe looked puzzled.

"Albert?" he queried.

I mumbled some unconvincing story about a friend from a neighbouring unit who had been killed. Mr. Thorpe was silent for a long moment.

"Albert was Tommy, wasn't he?" he said eventually.

I nodded. "How did you guess, sir?"

"It was just a hunch. There was something furtive about Tommy Atkins, and when you said 'Albert,' I remembered hearing McLean use that name. Are you writing to tell the poor woman of his death?"

"Yes, sir," I answered. "But no one knows Albert's address, so I'm going to send the letter to our school for forwarding."

"I see. And how were you going to get the letter past the censors?"

I hadn't thought that far ahead. Every letter posted by a soldier in France is read and censored so that no important information is given away. The censor would not allow even the details I had included.

"I hadn't thought of that, sir," I replied weakly.

"Well," Mr. Thorpe said, "you are but a lowly private and I am a mighty lieutenant. This gives me certain privileges. For instance, tomorrow I must go to Divisional Headquarters for a conference. Anything posted there escapes the censor. If you like, I will post your letter. I would like to add my own regrets at Tommy … Albert's death. I too believe that the poor woman should hear of her tragedy kindly, and the army is not known for its sensitivity.

"Of course, it would mean that I would have to read

your letter, but I promise not to change or delete anything without telling you."

"Thank you, sir," I said. "I am sure Albert would appreciate it."

I handed him the letter, and he left me to my thoughts.

There are two worlds now. In one, people like Albert's mother are sheltered from truth. In the other, people like Iain and me live it in all its horror. Will they ever come together again? If not, will I ever be able to go back to the other world? I don't know, but if there is to be any chance, my black dreams must cease first.

BRITISH FORCE SURRENDERS TO TURKS

Major-General Charles Townshend and his force of 8,000 men surrendered to the Turks in Kut. After holding out valiantly for 196 days, during which a relief on the Tigris River approached to within twenty miles, a lack of food and drinking water has forced this sad conclusion.

Tuesday, May 16, Pierregot

Met an old friend today. Some Canadians are billeted down the road. I was working on filling in a shell hole when I heard a familiar accent. It was Arthur Hewitt, whom I had last seen on Salisbury Plain. We could talk for only ten minutes, but Arthur managed to grouse about both the Canadian Ross rifle and the Colt machine gun. At least their rather bizarre and useless trenching tools have been recalled.

All Arthur's complaints were presented with good-natured irony, and our encounter thoroughly cheered me. I cannot wait to go to such an open, uncomplicated country.

Wednesday, May 17, Pierregot

Word is that we are to move up to near Ypres for further training. It will be a change, but maybe better the devil you know. The bad dreams continue.

Tuesday, May 23, near Ypres

This part of the line is much different from the friendly, quiet old Somme valley. Here there has been heavy fighting since the very first days of the war. We marched through Ypres this morning. The town is rubble, with narrow streets cleared between the ruins. The cathedral and cloth hall must have been imposing buildings — the cathedral is much larger than Paisley Abbey — but the shelling has reduced both to little more than burnt-out shells. A few civilians still live in the cellars and scratch some meagre existence amongst the ruins, but mostly the town is taken over by soldiers, either coming from the line or going to it. At all hours, shells crash at random. It really is a depressing place.

The feeling here is that war is the natural state of affairs — that it has been going on forever and will continue to do so. The less scarred landscape around the Somme is much more hopeful. Thank heavens it is there we will attack.

We are billeted in a small town near Ypres and will have several days of training in bombing and clearing dugouts. I think we have moved up here to create space for new units to experience the Somme country before the Big Push there. We, after all, are very familiar with it, having been there almost continuously since November.

The bright spot is that, once this training is over, we will go on leave — two whole weeks! Surely there will be an opportunity for a picnic in there somewhere. The leave and seeing you again, Anne, are what I live for, but it scares me. We have not spoken face to face for six months. Your letters have been wonderful, cheering me in some very low times, yet I cannot help but doubt. We last spoke of love and of spending our lives together. Of marriage and going to Canada. But it was so long ago it seems like a dream. Do you still feel the same? Your letters say so, but are you just being kind so as not to upset me?

I have changed. In these six months I have gone through things that have marked me. I shall never be able to look at the world — or my fellow man — in the same way again. Does war make us demons who can cheerfully kill our fellows, or are the demons only hidden at other times? I do not know. But the cheerful, enthusiastic, naïve boy that you said you loved half a year ago is dead. Will you be able to love his replacement?

Thursday, May 25, near Ypres

Hugh has taken well to bombing training. He relishes the thought that the dummy bombs we throw around now will one day be filled with explosives that will kill and maim rooms full of men.

"He does take some sick pleasure in killing, be it rats, Germans, Frenchmen or Irishmen," Iain agreed.

"Do you think Hugh would kill anyone in civilian life?" I asked.

"Who knows," he replied. "Maybe he would be a murderer. Maybe the threat of the law would keep him in check. But now that he has a taste of living without the law, will it curb him after this is all over?"

"Surely that applies to all of us," I added. "Millions of men torn from a normal, peaceful existence have been given guns and bombs. Their friends are killed before their eyes, and they are taught to kill other human beings. How are they ever going to go back to being bank clerks or carpenters?"

"I don't know," Iain said, "but the longer the war goes on, the more different people will become."

"Yes," I agreed. "Fortunately, the Big Push will put an end to it."

"Perhaps," Iain said uncertainly. "Right now, I'm looking forward to a good night's sleep that will bring me one day closer to two weeks' leave. Fourteen days of soft beds and Aunt Sadie's baking. I can't wait."

Neither can I.

Saturday, May 30, near Ypres

Bombing course finished today. We are now all experts, although no one took to it quite as Hugh did. We head back to the Somme tomorrow for a few days before leave. There is an expectation in the air. Very soon now, Kitchener's New Army will leave its trenches and show the world what it can do. But first, our picnic. No horrible dreams for several nights now.

Thursday, June 1, near Amiens

Back where we belong, but farther from the lines. Staggered leave has begun. Some men are away already. Iain and I will get our turn in a week or so. I can barely wait. Meanwhile, we practise the attack, on a replica of the ground we will take when the Big Push comes. Ours is to be against our old friend the Wonderworks, which will have been rendered harmless by our artillery. I have seen that land through the periscope a hundred times and, in peacetime, I could walk over for a cup of tea in ten minutes. Yet it is as foreign as China or Siberia and, until our artillery has done its work, as inaccessible as the moon.

Our tin helmets have arrived. Very smart. They are quite heavy, but they have a comfortable web lining. There is a shine to them, which Iain worries will glint in the low sun of our morning attack. All I worry about is losing mine.

Friday, June 2, near Amiens

More practice over mock battlefields — this time watched by the mighty generals on horseback. Haig is a small dapper man who sat ramrod-straight as we charged. Actually, our artillery will have done such a thorough job that charging will be unnecessary. We are to walk through the German lines: full packs, rifles at the slope across our chests, in line and regulation distance between men. We will advance at a stately pace over the demolished and deserted enemy strong points. High explosives will have destroyed the defences and killed the enemy or driven him insane, and shrapnel will have cut the barbed wire. It will be a glorious day. General Haig said as much when he addressed us briefly after our practice.

"With God's help, I feel hopeful for our upcoming offensive," he said. He has a Scottish accent, but a very upper-class one. As Iain said later, it sounds as if he has a mouthful of plums. "You men are in splendid spirits, and the wire will be well cut. Opportunities to use the cavalry will be aggressively sought after you break through into open country.

"I believe that fire-power is not the decisive factor in battle. Victory is won with morale and the bayonet, or the fear of it. Your morale will win through for the Empire. Good luck."

Beside me, Iain almost choked. "Morale, bayonets and cavalry!" He was whispering, but the anger in his voice was obvious. "The idiot's still fighting the Zulus.

How can he say that fire-power isn't important? God will need to help us, but I am sure the Germans feel that God is on their side, too."

Iain can be such a wet blanket. Fortunately, he had calmed down by the time we marched back to our billets. Still, he has been very quiet this evening. I shall not be downcast. This is what we came for, and we will do it. The only thing that makes this waiting bearable is the leave that draws ever closer.

FIFTEEN-MONTH ADVENTURE IN THE FROZEN SOUTH

Sir Ernest Shackleton has returned safely, relates a message from the South Atlantic. Crews at the remote whaling station on South Georgia in the Falkland Islands were astounded when three ragged men stumbled out of the mountainous interior of the island. After being out of touch for nearly two years, Shackleton has returned. Although unsuccessful in his attempt to cross the frozen Antarctic continent, and despite his ship being crushed by ice, Shackleton has not lost a single man on this epic of endurance. His first question upon reaching civilization was, Who won the war?

Saturday, June 3, near Amiens

How strange. Shackleton used to be my hero. I remember him setting off on that hazy weekend before the world erupted into war. How thrilled I was. But so much has happened. The heroes are here now, struggling against a human enemy rather than a natural one. How odd Shackleton's return must have been. He left Britain the weekend the war began and heard of it by telegraph in those heady days when victory appeared around the corner. Yet the war is still under way. But it will be over soon, and we are the heroes who will end it.

GREATEST NAVAL BATTLE IN HISTORY IN NORTH SEA

Sunday, June 4, near Amiens

News came today of a great naval engagement at Jutland. I can barely contain my excitement. This feels like the first days of the war — when I was a boy. What better prologue to our great advance than a great victory for the navy? True, the victory was not complete — the German fleet scuttled back to their protected harbour before Jellicoe and Beatty could finish them off — but let them just show their noses out in the open sea again!

I am finding Iain's negativity tiresome. When I said what a great victory Jutland was, he replied, "The Germans did run back to their harbours. But look at the losses. We had the advantage of surprise and superior numbers, yet more British ships and sailors lie at the bottom of the North Sea today than German."

I said too loudly, "I suppose next you will be saying that our Big Push will fail."

"I will not," he replied. "Our preparations are vast and well in hand as far as a lowly soldier can tell. But I do not believe it will be as easy as everyone is saying."

"Well, I think it will be easy, and I will not let you spoil the moment with your gloom."

"And neither you should," Iain went on with a smile. "Nor would I if I were going back to a beautiful girl and a picnic so long in the planning. Aunt Sadie is a lovely, sweet person, but hardly your Anne."

We both laughed. Who cannot be happy now that the end is in sight?

FRENCH CONTINUE TO HOLD ON AT VERDUN

Despite mounting casualties, the French forces continue to hold the high ground and many of the forts around the vital town of Verdun. Unsubstantiated reports that some French units have refused to return to the front lines and that others march forward bleating like sheep being taken to the slaughter are mere German propaganda. However, as the French continue to be heavily engaged, they can offer only slight support in our upcoming Big Push.

Wednesday, June 7, near Amiens

Two days and I shall be on my way to a fortnight's glorious leave. And just as well. I could not stand many more practice assaults on these mock trenches.

I talked briefly with Lieutenant Thorpe today. He found me reading, as is usual in my spare time. It was a poetry magazine, and I was struggling through a poem by an American called T. S. Eliot. Some of the language was vivid, but I hadn't a clue what he was talking about. I was just about to give up when Lieutenant Thorpe arrived.

"That is very dense stuff for a young lad," he said, peering over my shoulder.

"To be honest, sir, I don't understand a word of it."

Mr. Thorpe laughed. "I can't blame you. Some of this modern poetry can be very difficult. Have you ever tried writing poetry?"

I had never even thought of it.

"No, sir," I replied, "I'm no poet."

"Don't dismiss the idea just because Mr. Eliot writes difficult poems. You understand Mr. Kipling, don't you?"

"Yes, sir," I said, "but is that real poetry?"

"It is all real, and many more people read and derive pleasure from Mr. Kipling than from Mr. Eliot. In any case, read what you enjoy. Life is too short to do otherwise. And everyone has something of the poet in him."

With that, Lieutenant Thorpe left. Perhaps I will give it a try — as long as Hugh McLean never finds out!

LORD KITCHENER LOST

Field Marshal Lord Kitchener is dead. Britain's foremost soldier and the force behind the New Armies died in the icy waters off the Orkney Islands when HMS *Hampshire,* on which he was travelling to boost morale in Russia, went down with all hands after striking a mine. The nation mourns the loss of such a man, but his legacy lives on in the New Armies, poised even now to sweep forward to victory.

Thursday, June 8, near Amiens

What a tragedy. Kitchener of Khartoum will be immortalized as the great hero of this war. This army that Iain, and I, and Hugh and millions of others are a part of is Kitchener's creation, but his work is done. When we are victorious, it will be because of him, but his death will not hold us back. It is a shame, though, that the great man did not live to see our success in the coming offensive.

A pleasant evening today. I have found a quiet spot amongst some trees where I can sit, look forward to tomorrow and write in my diary. Perhaps if the mood takes me, I will try a few lines of verse.

There is a battalion of Bantams billeted beside us — men who want to fight but who are shorter than the army allows. They are in special units, that ...

Returning, We Hear the Larks

Sombre the night is.
And though we have our lives, we know
What sinister threat lurks there.

Dragging these anguished limbs, we only know
This poison-blasted track opens on our camp –
On a little safe sleep.

But hark! joy – joy – strange joy.
Lo! heights of night ringing with unseen larks.
Music showering on our upturned list'ning faces.

Death could drop from the dark
As easily as song –
But song only dropped,
Like a blind man's dreams on the sand
By dangerous tides,
Like a girl's dark hair for she dreams no ruin lies there,
Or her kisses where a serpent hides.

Best wishes,
Isaac Rosenberg

I have met a poet — a real poet: Mr. Isaac Rosenberg. I cannot wait to tell Mr. Thorpe and Iain.

I was sitting with my back to a tree, writing and enjoying the unusual silence, when I noticed a short figure coming through the trees. I assumed, correctly as it turned out, that he was one of the Bantams I was just writing about. He was bareheaded and wore a private's uniform. His face seemed cluttered with features slightly too large for it. Even the forehead beneath the receding black hairline was broad. But the overall effect was pleasant and the man smiled at me. I guessed his age at around twenty-five.

"Hello, lad," he said in a voice that betrayed a hint of a cockney accent from the east end of London. He crouched beside me and held out his hand. "Isaac Rosenberg," he said.

"Jim Hay," I replied, shaking his hand.

"You are a writer then?" he asked, eyeing my diary.

"Just a diary."

"Some great literature is 'just' diaries. I am a bit of a scribbler myself. Poetry as it happens."

Then I recalled his name. Lieutenant Thorpe had mentioned him in one of our poetry talks and rated him highly.

"Yes," I blurted out. "I have heard of you."

Rosenberg looked startled.

"Really?" he said. "That puts you in some very select company. True, I have published a slim volume of poems, *Youth* by title, but its total sales were ten copies. You did not purchase one, did you?"

"No, but my platoon commander, Lieutenant Thorpe, has mentioned you."

"So, you have literary discussions with your officers? What a rare army this is."

"Do you have any of your work with you?" I asked. "I should like to read some."

"Would you? I have it all with me. Up here," he said, pointing to his broad forehead. "Would you really like to hear some?"

"Yes," I said enthusiastically.

"Very well. Here is a fragment of something I am working on at present:

> *The darkness crumbles away —*
>
> *It is the same old druid Time as ever.*
>
> *Only a live thing leaps my hand —*
>
> *A queer sardonic rat —*
>
> *As I pull the parapet's poppy*
>
> *To stick behind my ear.*
>
> *Droll rat, they would shoot you if they knew*
>
> *Your cosmopolitan sympathies.*
>
> *Now you have touched this English hand*
>
> *You will do the same to a German —"*

I made him repeat it until I had it memorized.

"It is only a beginning," he said. "My idea is to put things in opposite, just as this war does. We live in the ground, just like the rats, but they are better than we at it. They can move about without fear, visiting friend and foe alike. We are bigger, stronger, more intelligent, but they will survive longer.

"I want to bring in poppies more, too — blood and death."

I didn't say anything. My mind was reeling with the images and with memories of Hugh torturing the rat.

"I have depressed you." He interrupted my thoughts.

"No, no," I protested, but he held up his hand.

"Well, I have something else," he said. "If I may write in your diary."

I handed him my diary, and he wrote out the poem about larks. When he had finished, he signed his name with a flourish.

"It is not so very cheerful," he said, "but I do not think this is the time or place for good cheer. And the larks are an image of freedom, at least. Let us hope that this army of poets can end the madness soon. Keep writing your diary, Jim Hay. Goodbye."

"Goodbye," I said as he walked away through the trees. Are we truly "an army of poets?" It is a powerful thought. Perhaps I shall try some verse … one day.

But now I must tell of my adventure to Iain and Mr. Thorpe. What a day!

CANADIANS SUFFER HEAVILY BUT HOLD THE LINE

Despite their trenches being devastated by the detonation of two huge German mines, Canadian soldiers in the Ypres salient held their own against concerted German assaults. Though pushed back to within two miles of the city itself, they resisted sternly.

Friday, June 9, afternoon,
Victoria Railway Station, London,

Here I am back on home ground. I have just said good-bye to Iain, who had to rush to get the train out west to his Aunt Sadie's. The overnight express to Scotland does not leave for a couple of hours yet.

I am sitting amongst my kit with my back against one of the ornate iron columns that support the glass roof of this echoing building. Yet less than twenty-four hours ago, my back was against a tree within sound of the guns, and I was talking with Isaac Rosenberg. Iain was not as impressed by my encounter as I would have hoped, and I did not have a chance to tell Lieutenant Thorpe. That will have to wait.

All around me is bustle. Trains from the south coast arrive continuously, bringing soldiers who are on leave or are wounded. Most still have the mud of France on their boots, and all look slightly stunned. London has been bombed by the Zeppelins, but life goes on much as was usual before the war. What is usual now is living below ground with the "queer sardonic rats," and the mud, guns and danger of imminent death. No wonder we soldiers are amazed. Some men shout and sing and boast of what they will do on leave; others march through the chaos of luggage and bodies, focused on their ultimate destination, where they can adjust at leisure; still others, like myself, sit around in imposed inactivity, adjusting as best we can.

I can barely believe that tomorrow I will be with you, Anne. I am thrilled and terrified all at once. I hope I can sleep on the train.

Friday, June 9, night, on the train somewhere north of London

I am taking refuge in my diary. Refuge from my companion in the compartment. He is a businessman on his way back to Yorkshire after concluding a profitable deal in the city. The problem is his constant chatter and insufferable enthusiasm for the war. I have tried every means I know to tell him I want only to sleep, but he refuses to take the hint. His talk is either about how successful his business is — he runs a factory that makes bombs for the troops — or about how noble our cause is. He makes me think of the delight Hugh would take in using one of this man's bombs to dismember another human being. There should not be profit in such work.

His second topic disgusts me, partly because the

man's attitude reminds me painfully of myself at the beginning of the war, gleefully taking pleasure in supposedly noble events that were merely overwhelming death and suffering. How would this pompous little profiteer react were he in a crumbling trench, in filthy, lice-ridden clothes, scared out of his wits by the bullets and explosions and gazing at the rotting body of a comrade poorly buried in the trench wall? If the shock did not kill him, he might have a right to talk of such things.

There is an unbridgeable gulf of experience between him and me. I am half his age, yet he is the child. I have seen and done things that he cannot understand and that I cannot explain to him. His concerns will remain his business and his profits, and I do not think those will ever be important to me. Will it be possible to bridge this gulf after the war is over? Will you understand, Anne?

I will try to sleep now.

Saturday, June 10, early morning, approaching Glasgow

I slept well despite all. No bad dreams. When I awoke, the sun was rising over the heather-clad hills and the annoying little man had gone.

We will arrive soon. I have washed and made myself look as presentable as possible. I intended to write more about how I am feeling, but my hand is shaking and I am more scared than I have ever been at the Front. I have decided that, if you do not love me, Anne, I shall return to the Front immediately. I could not bear to be near you otherwise. Not long now. I must try to relax!

Sunday, June 11, Paisley

I am the happiest person in the world! The sky is more blue for me; the birds sing more tunefully; the flowers smell sweeter. I feel as if I shall explode with sheer happiness. I need to sing. I want to dance.

What nonsense! But I cannot help it.

All my cares have fled. Anne loves me, and I have two wonderful weeks of bliss before me.

This is no use. The words rushing around my head look so stupid on the page. I will leave them in my head.

CANADIANS RETAKE MOUNT SORRELL IN DRAMATIC NIGHT BAYONET ATTACK

The Canadian troops that were so badly mauled but a few days ago have recaptured their old front-line trenches in one of the most spectacular attacks of the war so far. Under cover of darkness, without a massive artillery bombardment and with orders not to fire, they stormed the German positions and drove out the enemy.

Thursday, June 15, Paisley

I am calmer now. I am still the happiest person in the world, but it is a quieter joy. This is mostly thanks to Anne's father, who is a rock of sanity in the torrent of Anne's and my love. (I must be careful not to go overboard again.)

Anne and her father met me at the station last Saturday morning. It was an awkward moment. I think neither Anne nor I was certain how the other felt. Her father had to carry the conversation as we made our way back to the house. There, we had tea, but the atmosphere remained terribly strained for the rest of the morning. I washed and unpacked and joined the others in the parlour before lunch.

For a while we talked without actually saying anything. Even when Anne's father pointedly left us alone, we confined ourselves to strained small talk. How long we would have continued, I do not know. Fortunately, before we went in for lunch, Mr. Cunningham burst out, "For God's sake, you pair. Are you going to spend the whole two weeks pussyfooting around and not saying anything to each other? In case you hadn't noticed, there is a war on. Time is too precious to waste." He turned to me. "Now, Jim, Anne loves you. She has told me so until I am sick of hearing it."

Anne blushed scarlet, but her father raised his hand and she kept silent.

"And, Anne, it is obvious to me that Jim here still loves you. He has the look of a sick puppy to him, and I suspect that, were he not too shy, he would be grovelling at your feet."

It was my turn to blush.

"So, there it is, out in the open. You two love each other, and you haven't much time. There is a splendid cold lunch in the dining room, and I am going to enjoy it. I suggest that you speak seriously to each other. But don't make it too long if you wish some food left on the buffet."

With that, he strode out of the room. Anne and I stood, red-faced and stunned, staring after him. It was Anne who broke the silence. "He is right, you know. I do still love you."

My heart was pounding so much I felt light-headed. "I — I was so afraid you wouldn't," I stammered. "I love you."

We fell into an embrace and kissed. We didn't need to say anything after all.

When we eventually went in to lunch, Anne's father was tucking heartily into a plateful of cold cuts. He launched into conversation as if nothing had happened, saying how glad he was that I was back safely and how much he was looking forward to continuing our evening poetry readings.

I told him about meeting Rosenberg and promised to read the poem he wrote out for me. I feel as if I have truly come home.

In the afternoon, Anne and I got to know each other again. We have both changed, but I think it is mainly a maturing. War certainly forces one to grow up rapidly.

Since then, the days have been a bliss of rediscovering old haunts and each other. The town is somehow less vibrant than in that glorious lost summer of 1914. Many railings are down — the metal gone to the munitions factories. Clothes are drabber than I remember, and the lights are out at night for fear of Zeppelins. But the people are cheerful.

Anne's father has left us to our own devices except in the evenings, when we all talk and read aloud. Much of the talk is of Canada and how it will be the place to make a new life after all this is over.

Everything is idyllic — and on Sunday we will finally have our picnic. We must. It dare not rain. We will take the country bus out to a spot that I remember by the river. It is the perfect place and, even if we must sit beneath umbrellas, we shall have our picnic!

All this and only day five.

Sunday, June 18, Paisley

I am so very tired and happy, but could not sleep without recording something of the most wonderful day of my life.

Anne and I are married!

Not in the legal sense, but what does that matter? This afternoon, under the most perfect tree, by the most perfect stream, in this most perfect world, we made love.

Perhaps I should not write of such things. But why not? It is not wrong, although some prudes may say it is. How could something so beautiful be wrong?

We are one now and will always be so. I cannot even remember the war.

Tuesday, June 20, Paisley

My second week already. How can the time have flown so quickly?

Today we went to visit Mother's house. It is boarded up and to be sold. The proceeds of her estate, a reasonable sum it appears, will be put in trust until I reach my eighteenth birthday. The lawyers wanted to make it twenty-one, but Mr. Cunningham argued that I was already a soldier and I would have need of the money as soon as the war was over.

So it seems that Anne and I will be quite well off. We have long discussions about going to Canada and beginning anew.

Suddenly, Saturday and the train back to France loom large. I shall go — there is no doubt of that. The work must be done, and I have committed to seeing it through. But the strings holding me here are much stronger than they were when I first went overseas.

What if I do not come back? It would be a cruel fate indeed to die when my life is opening up so wonderfully, but even in the hour of our great victory, I could be one of the unlucky ones.

Wednesday, June 21, Paisley

Anne and I are to be married! I stammered out a proposal this morning as we walked in the sunshine. I was not very romantic and I have no ring as yet, but Anne accepted. We will marry on Friday.

Anne wanted to wait until after the war, and I would have liked to have Iain stand up for me, but it has to be now. For one thing, the war may still take months, and a lot can happen in that time. Also, if we are married and something happens to me, my inheritance will automatically go to Anne. But nothing will happen to me, and the money will buy us a farm and a new life in Canada.

Thursday, June 22, Paisley

Frantic day. Anne and I have bought a ring. She has a new dress, and I have bought a suit, even though it would be perfectly acceptable to wed in my uniform. But I do not wish to be reminded that this war will drag us apart on the first day of our married life. Mr. Cunningham has been wonderful, organizing countless details and picking apart countless bureaucratic knots. We could not have managed without him.

In the midst of all this, I performed a task that I promised myself I would do, but that I have been postponing — I went to visit Albert's mother. She had received my letter (thank you, Lieutenant Thorpe) and was most grateful. She was red-eyed throughout and wanted only to be reassured that Albert had not suffered. I stuck with the story in my letter, so she will never know how he really died. What is one small lie in all this horror, especially if that lie brings peace to a lonely woman?

This evening, Anne's father read "A Valediction: Forbidding Mourning," by John Donne. He chose it for us, as it is about having "no teare-floods nor sigh-tempests" on lovers' parting. It talks of two lovers' souls not breaking at separation, but thinning and stretching "like gold to ayery thinnesse beate." I shall carry that image with me.

Tomorrow Anne and I shall marry. What a wonder!

Saturday, June 24, on the train heading south

I am a married man — still weeks shy of eighteen years old. I am married and returning to war. What a strange time this is.

Iain sits across from me. Anne's father telegraphed him at his Aunt Sadie's and told him of our great event. Iain got the overnight train and arrived on our doorstep on Friday morning, in time to stand beside me. Apparently, Aunt Sadie insisted that he come, even though he was loath to leave her early. She is a wonderful person and I shall be eternally grateful to her. Iain's presence made my day complete.

The wedding ceremony was brief and clinical, but even that could not dampen our joy. We have promised that, after the war, we shall have a proper ceremony in a church, with flowers and bridesmaids and all. But for now, a civil ceremony and a lunch in the Royal Hotel. We returned home to find that Mr. Cunningham had made up the master bedroom for us as man and wife.

To think that a mere two weeks ago I was on a train trying to ignore the dreadful businessman, lonely and plagued by doubts. That now seems so silly. I AM MARRIED TO ANNE! I can still hardly believe it.

It was cruel to leave this morning, but it will not be for long. Our attack to end the war must be soon, and then I shall return to my new life. I am so happy.

CANADIAN SOLDIER CITED FOR BRAVERY

A Canadian soldier, Arthur Hewitt, has been recommended for the Military Medal for an act of extraordinary, unselfish bravery in the trenches of France.

On the night of June 14th last, as the Canadians were attacking to retake their old positions on Mount Sorrell, Private Hewitt and his unit successfully cleared a stretch of enemy trench. They were preparing to attack the next trench when a lobbed grenade landed amongst Private Hewitt's section. An explosion in such a confined space would have killed several men and injured the others. Without thought for his own safety, Private Hewitt threw his body on top of the grenade. It exploded, killing him instantly.

Undoubtedly, Private Hewitt's prompt action saved the lives of several of his comrades. His name is being put forward for the newly instituted Military Medal, which recognizes individual acts of bravery.

Private Hewitt was from Gravenhurst, Ontario.

Sunday, June 25, Pierregot

Back in our old haunts. The shock was terrible. The bombardment in preparation for our great attack began yesterday, and it is deafening, even this far from the Front. At night, the sky is lit with the high arcs of shells, heavy machine gun bullets and star flares. It is like a fireworks display for the gods.

The landscape has changed dramatically. Roads and light railways have sprung up everywhere, and the countryside is dotted with dumps of supplies and shells. It is very encouraging to see the mass of equipment supporting us. Less encouraging are the

Casualty Clearing Stations everywhere. Let us hope they remain empty.

It is strange how rapidly I have adapted. Of course I miss Anne and my new life at home dreadfully, but the world here, for all its change, is so familiar that I do not need to think — I simply exist, and there is an attraction in that. There is also an air of expectation to everything we do. This is what we joined up for — what we were born for, it seems. I can almost touch the excitement around me.

Tomorrow we work and rest here before moving closer to our starting positions. No one feels like resting, even though we shall have no sleep tomorrow night, so we have arranged a football game against the 17th.

The copy of the *Daily Mail* I picked up in London contained news of the death of my Canadian friend, Arthur Hewitt. He did not strike me as the medal-winning type. I suppose you can never tell.

THUNDER OF THE GUNS AUDIBLE

So great is our bombardment in France, the most intense in history, that it is clearly audible as a dull roar all along the south coast of England. It is even said that, when the wind is from the right quarter, the guns can be heard in London.

Monday, June 26, Pierregot

I am just snatching a few moments to write before we set out this evening. The promised football game got under way this afternoon. All went well until just after half-time. The 17th were ahead one goal to nil and were attacking in force. There was so much shouting and cheering that we did not hear the large shell arrive. It must have been a stray, as we have never been shelled here before.

I was moving in to tackle their winger, who was preparing to cross the ball, when I was deafened and we were both blown off our feet. I was stunned and totally confused. My ears were ringing and red spots danced before my eyes.

The shell — it must have been a 5.9 or bigger — had landed behind our goal. Fortunately, there had been no spectators close by, but our goalkeeper had not been so lucky. His body lay, impossibly bent and entangled in the goal netting, beside the penalty spot.

Hugh was sitting nearby, cursing loudly and looking down at his legs. They were a mess, the right one almost completely severed.

I was relieved to see Iain on the far side of the pitch, looking dazed but otherwise unharmed.

So, Hugh will not have his chance to wreak havoc on the enemy after all. If he survives, he will never walk again, let alone fight. What a life shall he have, trapped in a wheelchair, suffering the interminable kindness of people with legs? Nonetheless, I hope he survives the hospital. He was still conscious and as foul-mouthed as ever when they stretchered him away. It seems such a tragedy to lose men so pointlessly, on the eve of our great victory.

We are being called to form up. It is going to be a long night, and now it is raining.

CHEAPER AUTOMOBILES AVAILABLE SOON

American industrialist Henry Ford is in the midst of a plan to make automobiles available to many people who now rely on more expensive horse-drawn carriages. The effects of this plan should be greatest in the United States and in countries such as Canada and Australia, where the distance between communities is so great.

Tuesday, June 27, Authuille

A battered village south of Thiepval Wood. From here we shall go into the front lines. Zero hour is set for Thursday. Rain showers all day. The ground is unpleasantly muddy in places.

I was quite worried that my dream of the black dog would return last night. He seems to come after a shock — witnessing Crozier's execution or some trench horror — and I thought Hugh's tragedy might invite it back. But I slept well. Perhaps I have seen the last of it.

This close to the Front, the effect of the bombardment is awesome. It is as if we are beneath an umbrella of steel. One can even follow the flights of individual

15-inch howitzer shells. Although the shelling is heaviest in the morning and evening, the roar is continuous. At night, the sky is brightly lit and the chatter of long-range machine-gun fire adds to the din. The German response is minimal. It is even possible to walk about in the open without fear. Many of us do this to watch the bombardment. In the distance, the enemy trenches stand out as white lines on the hillside. There are patches of yellow weed and the bright red of poppies amongst the green fields. It is very colourful — highlighted by the smoke of our exploding shells, puffs of yellow, black or white. They look quite harmless, although not to the Germans beneath them.

Above us, the air force photographs the damage done by the shelling and keeps German planes away from our preparations. How delightful it must be to soar like a bird. But I would not be elsewhere right now. This is our moment.

SOLDIERS' SUPERSTITIONS

It is unlucky for thirteen to sit down for a meal when there are rations for only seven.

It is unlucky to take the third light for a cigarette.

It is unlucky to drop your rifle on the sergeant's foot.

It is unlucky to hear a lecture on the glorious history of your regiment — it means a big attack is coming.

It is considered very unlucky to be killed on a Friday.

Wednesday, June 28, Authuille

Postponement! Forty-eight hours. It is because of the rain and to give the artillery a chance to work on the German wire. Apparently, it is not cut in places. The news reached us as we were forming up this afternoon to move into our jumping-off trench. Now we are settled back in our old billets. The waiting will be difficult. Iain seems particularly down at the news.

"We had shells enough for five days. Now they must last for seven."

"So what?" I asked. "It will just make the Germans' lives more unpleasant."

"Perhaps," Iain said with a frown, "but if the rate of shelling decreases, the Germans are going to take advantage of it — repairing their trenches and moving fresh men into their line. It will just make our work harder."

"Iain!" I exclaimed. "Can you never see the positive? There are no German trenches or men to fill them. They have all been blown to bits. We have not heard a sound from the German artillery because it has also been blown to bits."

FIGHTING AROUND VERDUN WINDS DOWN

Due to exhaustion on both sides, the intensity of the fighting around Verdun is waning, without a clear victor. To date, German casualties are estimated at 281,000; French at 315,000.

Thursday, June 29, Authuille

This is the day we should have been attacking. Instead, here we still are. The waiting is hard. We are to be in the first wave. Ten per cent of the men are to be kept in reserve. Iain says it is to form the nucleus of a new battalion if we don't come back. He can be so depressing.

In any case, we will be a little more than 700 strong. That should be plenty to take over our short stretch of empty trenches. Tomorrow night we shall move up to our jumping-off points in no man's land. We are to go over the top at 7:30 on Saturday morning. What a great day in British history July 1, 1916, will be!

Friday, June 30, Authuille

It is late afternoon and we move off within the hour. We are all laden with at least sixty pounds of equipment, but our spirits are so high it feels like nothing.

Lieutenant Thorpe approached me this afternoon and offered me a spot in the ten per cent staying behind.

"It is no dishonour," he said. "Someone must, after all."

But I have waited too long for this moment.

Once it became clear that he could not persuade me, we had a long chat in the sunshine. Not at all like officer and private, but more like two old friends. I told him of the meeting with Isaac Rosenberg and showed him the poem written in my diary. He told me of his family in England and the grand life they led before the war — fox hunting and taking tea with famous men. I told him of Father's sacrifice, Mother's illness and of you, Anne, and our hurried marriage. I quite surprised myself with my eloquence.

"You love her very much?" Mr. Thorpe asked when I had finished.

"Yes, I do," I replied.

"You are a lucky pair," he said. "Keep your head down tomorrow and stick close by me. How is your diary coming along?"

"I write whenever I can." I was surprised by the question.

"Good. You have spent a lot of time on it. It may be a valuable document one day."

I laughed, but he was serious.

"We live in extraordinary times. What we say and do and think, while insignificant at the moment, may be important in time. What will you do with it during the attack?"

I hesitated, as I had decided to carry it with me. It is against the rules, but I have no way of knowing how far we will advance and when I will be able to return to claim it. Besides, I wish to record this great event as quickly as possible.

Lieutenant Thorpe noticed my hesitation. "Are you taking it with you?" he asked.

I nodded.

"Well, you haven't mentioned that to me. And make sure no one else finds out."

"Yes. Thank you."

"I would like to read it one day," he said, "after this is all over."

"Certainly," I replied, "but you will be horribly bored."

"I think not," he said, standing to leave. "Oh, and make sure your name is on the diary." Then he added, almost as an afterthought, "And write your Anne's name and address inside the cover."

I was going to ask why, but he walked away rapidly. It is a sensible precaution, in case anything happens to me, but I wonder if Lieutenant Thorpe thinks we will have as easy a time of it as everyone expects. We will find out soon enough.

I love you, Anne.

FIRST REPORTS ENCOURAGING

Initial communications from our forces attacking on the Somme River suggest significant advances and large numbers of prisoners taken. Cavalry units are standing by in reserve to exploit the breakthrough. No word yet on casualties.

Saturday, July 1, 7:00 a.m., front line

I am back in our familiar stretch of front line, but the trench is crowded in preparation for the attack. We have just been issued our rum ration and, for once, I enjoyed it. The warmth was welcome, and it helped calm the butterflies in my stomach. Everyone is tense. Some sit on the fire-step in thoughtful silence. Others chatter inconsequentially. Many are writing notes and letters to loved ones, so my scribbling will go unnoticed.

The shelling eased overnight as we were struggling into position, but it has redoubled and the noise is almost unbearable. I hope it is doing its job. The sun lies low on the horizon behind what is left of the German lines. The narrow strip of sky above the trench is the most perfect blue. I can see birds soaring across, blissfully oblivious. What a lovely day it would be for a picnic.

Was our picnic only two weeks ago, Anne? It was the best day of my life. The red blanket spread in the mottled shade of the chestnut tree, and the ham and bread in the hamper we carried across the field. The heavy, warm air filled with the smells of the country and the murmuring hum of insects, busy at the meadow flowers. The ants advancing between the knife-edged blades of grass towards the blanket — planning their attacks on the crumbs we dropped. The stream gurgling over the stones and the curious cow chewing thoughtfully. It is almost more vivid than the reality around me. I suppose that's the way I want it to be. The mind is a strange thing.

Your hand felt so soft and cool — mine sweaty and hot. When you looked at me, I was sure you were looking into my soul. What did you see there? And when I was so overwhelmed that I almost cried, you were understanding. You smiled and placed my hand against your cheek. I can feel your hand cupping the back of my head and drawing me forward. I heard a lark singing then, and the rest of the world ceased to exist.

I am frightened. I don't want to die on such a beautiful morning. I want to live, go back to you, Anne. I want to take you on that steamer to our new life in Canada, an eternal picnic beside the lake. My boots are Canadian, did I tell you? Canada sent two million pairs, all the same size. Does everyone in Canada have the same-sized feet? Maybe we won't be allowed in. A shame about Arthur Hewitt. I should like to have visited with him in Canada.

Iain is beside me, a mirror image: same khaki jacket, trousers, backpack and tin helmet; same Lee Enfield rifle, shorter barrelled because they were designed to be carried by cavalrymen — have I told you that? Same bayonets, bombs, water bottle and first-aid kits. We all look the same, except Lieutenant Thorpe — he doesn't have a tin helmet, pack or rifle. He is gazing intently at the watch on his left wrist. He has a whistle in his right hand. His lips are moving, probably reciting poetry.

It's funny, Anne, what I am frightened of is so simple — in a few minutes I will become one of the first human beings in two years to stand upright in daylight on this patch of France. A week ago, I would have been dead in an instant, but that shrapnel and high explosive that have been tearing over my head for days are just so I can stand up. All the agonizing hours of drill and marching, the cold uncomfortable billets in draughty barns or open fields, the lice, the mud, the fear — everything leads to this one moment when I shall stand up in the open. Strange, isn't it?

The guns have stopped. The silence is so thick it is like being under water. I can hear a bird, high-pitched and liquid, a fragile sound after the guns. I wonder if it's a lark, like the one on our picnic?

It's almost time. I love you, Anne. Wish me luck.

July 1, later

Oh Anne! Anne! Anne! It has all gone so horribly wrong. We did not even get to the German wire. We tried. Iain tried so hard that he will never try anything again. Should I keep trying? I don't know. I didn't want to die. Help me, Anne. Please!

If only I could stop shaking and concentrate. But the guns won't let me. The noise is awful. There is blood on my face. I think I have been unconscious. I am going mad!

No! I mustn't think that. I must concentrate. I will concentrate. I will tell you what has happened. I am in a shell hole in no man's land. I don't know how long I have been here. From the sun, I think it is still morning. There are three others with me. Two are dead and the third is dying. He moans all the time. His face … I try not to look at him. I must concentrate on remembering accurately.

I had barely time to put my diary away when Mr. Thorpe blew his whistle. It sounded awfully loud. Suddenly we were all scrambling up the trench wall, Mr. Thorpe first.

"Come on, boys!" he shouted. "You've been resting down there long enough. There's work to be done."

I threw my rifle over the parapet and scrambled up after it. I was terrified when I stood up. I felt so exposed, so vulnerable. I expected to be shot any moment — but nothing happened. I looked around properly for the first time. I could see the shell holes and the German trenches. Ahead, black puffs of smoke indicated where our shells were falling. There was grass at my feet. There was even an occasional tree still standing. Behind the Wonderworks, I could see a road, a small wood and a cluster of distant houses.

I began to walk towards them, but Iain grabbed my arm.

"Hey," he said, "don't forget your rifle."

What kind of soldier goes into battle and forgets his rifle?

Mr. Thorpe was getting us organized: straight lines, six feet apart, two platoons to every 200 yards, rifles held across our chests. The second wave 20 yards back.

"Come on, lads," he said. "Form up. Look lively. Regulation distance, eyes front. Hurry now, let's not give them any chance to recover."

The instructions were simple: we were to walk at a steady pace over the destroyed German wire and demolished trenches, clear out their dugouts and hold them against any counter-attack. Then the second phase of the attack would come over, pass through the first and secure the day's objectives. They were the ones who might have to do some fighting. I was relieved that our job was so easy, but envious too.

We walked forward slowly. After three steps I was sweating. It was hard work with all that equipment hanging off me. There were thousands of us, all in a neat row, stretching off to left and right. It looked so impressive. I could hear bagpipes, and there was a tiny black figure in the distance kicking a football.

"Keep together." "Not so fast on the left." "Steady."

Lieutenant Thorpe's reassuring voice echoed along the line. He was right in front of me, looking to both sides over his shoulders and waving his revolver in the air. All of a sudden, he stopped walking and knelt down. I thought he must have dropped something — probably his Keats. That's the only thing he would stop for.

I was about to ask if I could help look for it, but he just said, "Go on."

It was a bit confusing, but we had been told not to stop for any reason. So I kept going.

For a while there was no one in front of me. Then I saw figures emerging from the ground, like rabbits coming out to feed. They were kneeling and aiming rifles at me. In front of them, I could see the sun glinting off the barbed wire. Something was wrong. I thought I was going to throw up. The soldiers and the wire shouldn't have been there. There was a machine gun too. It made a heavy *tack tack tack* sound, rather like Mother's sewing machine, but deeper.

I looked along the line of soldiers. Some seemed to be stopping for a rest. They just sat or lay down. I thought maybe they were picking up souvenirs, but there was a definite pattern: they sat down one by one, along the line, in the sunshine — first one man, then his neighbour, then his neighbour. I couldn't work out what was happening. I turned to ask Iain, but he just gave a soft grunt and sat down as well. He looked surprised. I called his name and asked what was wrong, but the only reply was a gurgle. I crouched and reached round behind him, to help him lie down. Iain's back beneath his pack was wet. When I brought my hand back, it was all red and sticky. It was then I noticed the line of neat, round holes crossing his chest.

I think I screamed.

Iain tried to speak, but only blood came out. He sighed.

I am not clear on what happened next. I think I said something about the stretcher bearers being along soon.

Oh Anne, Iain is dead. He looked so peaceful lying there in the grass. I must tell Aunt Sadie. She would want to know he was peaceful.

I closed Iain's eyes and then kept walking. I couldn't think of anything else to do.

There were khaki heaps, like piles of dirty laundry, all around. Some were groaning or trying to crawl, but most just lay silent and still. The rest of the men were ahead of me, about twenty of them near the German wire. They were looking for a way through. There was none. Eventually the machine gun found them and they too lay down.

The second wave was all around me now. They were in lines, too, but ragged and their momentum carried me forward. I looked back, but I couldn't tell which heap was Iain.

The first shell exploded in front of me and to my right. It was quite beautiful. A deep red flash in the core. It rose into the air, hung for a second and collapsed back on itself. I felt the ground shake.

Soon shells were exploding all around me. The three men in front of me disappeared in a red flash. Our sergeant was staggering back, holding the stump where his left arm used to be. He kept asking, "Where are the boys?" Over and over.

The smell made me want to retch. The explosive is so acrid it hurts your eyes and throat. I stumbled about, completely alone, in the smoke and the smell and the noise.

Then something hit me on the head. It felt like the time I was in goal, diving for a low ball — the centre forward kicked me in the head and I saw stars for hours. Whatever it was knocked my helmet clean off. I think it was a piece of a shell, but it could have been a bullet.

I came to in this shell hole. I'm alive, Anne. My head hurts something terrible and I have this horrible ringing in my ears. I think they are bleeding a bit. Most of the blood on my face comes from where I was hit on the head. It's just a scratch, but I will have a nice bruise to show you. I wonder …

I must have blacked out for a while. The sun is farther round in the sky and the wounded man isn't groaning anymore. I think he is dead. They are all dead: Tom McDonald, Albert, Arthur Hewitt, Lieutenant Thorpe, Father, Mother, Iain. There is no one left except you. I am so lonely. Don't ever leave me, Anne.

There's something I have to do. It's important, but I cannot think what it is. What — I'm so tired.

THE BLACK DOG IS BACK.

I slept and he returned. But this time the dream finished. Now I know what I must do.

The black dog leaped from the river, bounded past

you and attacked me like before, and I couldn't move. But then, when I saw you, talking as if nothing happened, I realized that I had to fight the dog; otherwise, it would turn and attack you, too. I managed to stand and hit the dog. It cried in pain and fled back to the river. I felt brave and proud, and I wanted to tell you what I had done — but you were gone. Vanished. Then I saw Aunt Sadie, standing on a hill, beckoning. I started running towards her. I had to tell her something, but as hard as I ran, I couldn't get any closer. Eventually, I got to a large port. There was a ship and Aunt Sadie was on it. You and your father were beside her, and you were all beckoning to me. It was the ship for Canada, Anne. Now I know what I have to do. I must see Aunt Sadie and tell her about Iain. Then we will both come and get you and your father and go to Canada. It will be wonderful.

I'll see you soon, Anne. We are going to have such a wonderful life. I love you, Anne.

COMMUNIQUÉ

In the confusion attending the recent attacks along the Somme River, significant numbers of men have become separated from their units. Most can be expected to find their way back over the succeeding few days. However, some men of the weaker sort are using the opportunity to abscond. Failing in their duty, such men must be considered the worst kind of deserters.

When these men are apprehended, they must be disciplined in the strongest manner possible. The army must not be seen to tolerate this behaviour.

Tuesday, July 4 (I think)

I am in a shed with a guard. I don't know where the shed is, but the guns sound distant, so I must be behind the lines. I only remember walking through a battle, someone shouting my name, soldiers marching, horses, guns, a voice asking where I was going. I don't even remember writing in my diary in the shell hole. The last thing I remember clearly is our picnic.

The guard said I was found walking along a road and that I refused to state what I was doing or where my unit was. I know what I was doing — I was going to get you and your father and Aunt Sadie. We are going to Canada. But I cannot tell them that — it's our secret.

I know this is difficult to read, but I cannot stop my hand shaking. I also seem to cry for no reason. I don't think I have slept in a long time. I am too scared.

Wednesday, July 5, Bouzincourt

Dearest Anne: I feel better today. I slept some last night and that helped, although I was plagued by nightmares. Not the black dog — he is gone, I think. But dreams of everyone I have lost: Father, marching and waving; Mother, polishing silver; poor Albert with half his face missing; Hugh cursing his lost leg; and Iain with neat holes across his chest. And all the others — blown apart and destroyed. I wake in a cold sweat and cannot get back to sleep.

I still cry, and loud noises make me jump, but the shaking has eased a bit.

Anne, they are going to court-martial me for desertion. I didn't desert. Perhaps it was the knock on the head or perhaps it is Mother's madness in me. But I didn't desert. I shall tell them that, and they will send me to hospital until I am better. Then we can go to Canada. I am only very sorry that I couldn't tell Aunt Sadie what happened to Iain. I cannot remember the attack, but I have my diary and I see Iain die in my dreams.

The court martial will be on Friday.

Thursday, July 6, Bouzincourt

The black dog returned last night. The dream was the old one where I could not move. I awoke again in a sweat, certain that the dog would tear out my throat. What does it mean? Am I mad? I am so scared.

News today that Mr. Thorpe will be coming to my court martial. He was only wounded and, against doctor's orders, is leaving hospital to be here. Now I know everything will be fine tomorrow. If only I could sleep.

Friday, July 7, Bouzincourt

The court martial is over. It lasted only two hours — not long to decide a life. The court officers had the cleanest uniforms and shiniest buttons I have seen in a long time. I wanted to shout at them and throw mud and spray Iain's blood on their obscene cleanliness.

Lieutenant Thorpe spoke for me. Although he looked pale and weak in his wheelchair, he was very eloquent. He said that I was a good soldier, despite being so young. He said I was "sensitive." Imagine that. He said the knock on my head had made me confused, that I didn't know what I was doing and must have wandered. He's wrong, of course. I knew exactly what I was doing and why, but it's our secret, remember.

In any case, I don't think anything he said made a difference. They found me guilty. But Lieutenant Thorpe says that lots of death sentences are given out in wartime. Almost all are commuted to a dishonourable discharge. That will be fine. We just won't tell anyone in Canada.

I love you, Anne. I will be home soon.

Sunday, July 9, Bouzincourt

Dearest Anne: The decision of the court martial has been confirmed by General Haig. He said that soldiers who avoid their comrades' dangers cannot be tolerated. What nonsense — all my comrades are dead — I avoid their dangers simply by living. But not for long. I am to be shot tomorrow at dawn.

Monday, July 10, Bouzincourt

Darling Anne: The sky is lightening to the east and they will be coming for me soon. I am scared, very scared, but I will not make a fool of myself.

Lieutenant Thorpe is with me. He has been here all night. If I cannot have you beside me, and now that Iain is dead, there is no one I would rather have with me. He has been very kind. He is to be invalided home — they doubt if his leg will ever heal properly — and has promised to visit you and to get my diary to you. Meanwhile, he will write.

I feel strangely peaceful. The shaking has almost stopped. I slept for a couple of hours last night and was untroubled by the black dog or the dead. I still have very little memory of the attack and realize that it was silly to try to reach Aunt Sadie and take her and you to Canada. Maybe I was mad, like Mother. Perhaps this is for the best.

Anne, please remember me fondly and keep me in a little part of your heart — that shall be my immortality — but get on with your life. Find someone else and live — that's what's important. I will miss our dreams of life together in Canada, but at least we had our picnic.

It is a beautiful morning. Even the guns sound more distant than usual.

They are coming for me. I hope I make a good end.

I love you, Anne. Always have.

Goodbye, my love.

July 14, 1916
Bouzincourt

My Dear Mrs. Hay,

By the time you receive this, you will already know Jim's fate. I know what a horrible shock it must have been, especially considering the manner of his death. Like most things in this life, Jim's fate was not simple, as the enclosed diary will show. It is a remarkable document and he asked me specifically to forward it to you in its entirety. All I can add is a description of that final dawn.

I spent the night of July 9 with Jim, as every condemned soldier is allowed a "soldier's friend" to comfort him. Jim had been very distraught and obviously confused over the previous days, but as the night wore on, he calmed. By morning, the Jim I had grown to know and respect over the previous year and a half had returned. We talked of many things that night and, perhaps, if I come to visit you (I am to be invalided home within the next few days), I could share some of my memories.

The morning of July 10 was sunny, and Jim appeared to derive comfort from that. As they took him outside, he looked all around, as if trying to fix a final image of this

*world in his mind. Without protest, Jim allowed himself
to be sat in the chair, have his hands tied behind his
back and have the buff envelope pinned over his heart.
He complained only when the young officer in charge
offered the blindfold, and that was merely a brief shake
of the head.*

*The men in the firing party were from the 16th
HLI, but none were from F Company — not enough
unwounded survivors could be found.*

*As the firing party formed up, Jim looked across at
me and gave me a smile, which I returned. Then he
gazed upwards to the blue sky. It really was such a
beautiful summer day. The sun was shining and wisps of
dawn mist still clung to the ground. The blue of the sky
was magnificent, so bright, so vibrant. It was a colour no
artist has ever been able to capture.*

*As the squad prepared, I watched Jim closely. He
appeared to be searching the sky for something and was
frowning and tense. As the officer gave the order "Aim," a
lark flew across Jim's view. He visibly relaxed as he
watched its free flight. You could hear the lark singing,
and Jim smiled. His last words were "It's a perfect day for
a picnic."*

That was the end.

Please do not think Jim a coward. No one who has not suffered in this war can understand the extraordinary pressures it puts on a young man.

There is little more I can add other than to restate that I shall be returning home soon and would very much like to meet with you and your father. Jim told me much about you, and I almost feel I know you. He was, I think, a very lucky man. I can be reached by army post.

Please accept my deepest regrets and condolences. Jim was a fine soldier and my friend.

Yours in sorrow,

Robert P. Thorpe, Lieutenant.

My birthday gift — from my great-grandfather. As I folded Lieutenant Thorpe's letter, I noticed something written on the back of the last page. The handwriting was the same as in the letter at the beginning. It was addressed to me.

Dear Jim,

If you have got this far, you now understand something of young Jim Hay. But before you close this book and get on with your life, there is one more thing I have to tell you.

I, too, fought in Jim Hay's war. Unlike Jim, I was an officer, although I don't think I was a very good one — my head was too full of poetry and romantic ideals. Perhaps I might have become a better soldier, but I was wounded and invalided home. I tried to return to my family, but their life seemed so empty and frivolous after what I had seen that I couldn't settle.

I went to an address in Scotland that a young soldier had given me. The people there were most kind. They took me in and we became very close. The soldier's widow was pregnant, and you must know that in those days, single mothers, even the widows of soldiers, had a difficult time. To have a man around, even a wreck like I was, helped.

In any case, with time, the woman came to love me and I her. It was not the wild romantic love of my poetry, nor was it the passion she had known with her soldier, but it was as much as a widowed mother and a crippled, disillusioned poet could hope for.

We married and, after the war was over, settled in Canada. It was a happy life, I think, even though we had no children.

I suppose by now you have guessed that I was Lieutenant Thorpe and the young soldier's widow was Anne. The child she was carrying when I met her, Jim Hay's son, was your grandfather.

So, it is Jim Hay who is your great-grandfather — although I certainly love you as my own. This diary and his letters to Anne, which she inserted in it, are his gift to you. Please treasure it for all our sakes.

Robert Thorpe

HISTORICAL NOTE

On July 1, 1916, the British army suffered its worst day in history. Almost 20,000 men died and a further 40,000 were wounded. Thirty-two battalions suffered more than 500 casualties each, some in as little as half an hour, and almost all before noon. The 16th Battalion, Highland Light Infantry (Glasgow Boys' Brigade), existed, but there was no F Company. It was raised over a few days in August/September 1914. Seven hundred and fifty strong, the 16th went over the top on July 1, 1916. Five hundred and eleven men became casualties. Not one man made it past the German wire.

The Battle of the Somme dragged on into the fall at a cost of more than one million casualties on both sides. The village of Thiepval, where Jim and the 16th Highland Light Infantry were headed on July 1, was not captured until September 27, by which time it was little more than a smear of brick dust.

The First World War was finally over by Christmas — 1918. It took nearly 10 million lives, one of them Isaac Rosenberg's. He was shot while on night patrol on April 1, 1918 — April Fool's Day.

The casualty figures also include 327 British and Empire soldiers who were shot at dawn by their own side for a range of offences including desertion, disobedience, threatening a senior officer and casting away arms. James Crozier was one. After the war, his body was moved from Mailly-Maillet to Sucrerie Military Cemetery at Colincamps, where he rests today. Of the men shot during the war, at least 49 were under twenty-one years of age, and 32 had no legal representation at their trial. Of those executed, 211 were English, 38 were Scottish, 24 Irish, 13 Welsh, 5 New Zealanders, 1 South African and 25 Canadians. The Australian government did not allow the British army to execute a single one of its men.

The things that happened to Jim Hay did happen, but not all to one person. They are taken from many people's experiences. Many stories, from the battalion saying goodbye to Aunt Sadie on the railway platform to the shell landing during the football game, are found in the diaries, letters and histories of the 15th, 16th and 17th Highland Light Infantry Battalions.

ACKNOWLEDGEMENTS

The Imperial War Museum in London, England, preserves thousands of diaries, letters and histories written by men who fought and died in Jim Hay's war. The staff there were immensely helpful in assisting me to ferret out the stories that might have happened to Jim.

There is a book about the day that Jim Hay went over the top, called *The First Day on the Somme*, by Martin Middlebrook. There are also a host of interesting people who look after the vast cemeteries and monuments that mark where the front lines ran through France. They, and the graves and plaques they tend, also tell stories.

This is Jim Hay's tale, but it is told as well as it is in large part because of the attentions of Charis Wahl, who edited it.